Barton Orville Aylesworth

Thirteen

And twelve others

Barton Orville Aylesworth

Thirteen
And twelve others

ISBN/EAN: 9783337177164

Printed in Europe, USA, Canada, Australia, Japan

Cover: Foto ©Andreas Hilbeck / pixelio.de

More available books at **www.hansebooks.com**

"THIRTEEN"

AND TWELVE OTHERS

From the Adirondacks and Elsewhere.

BARTON O. AYLESWORTH.

———

St. Louis:
CHRISTIAN PUBLISHING COMPANY,
1892.

THIS little volume is faithfully inscribed to the Students and Faculty of Drake University, whose loyalty and efficiency have made my duties the most pleasant of my life.

THE AUTHOR.

DRAKE UNIVERSITY,
Des Moines, Iowa.

CONTENTS.

Braving the Pagan superstition that Thirteen is an unlucky number, I send this hopeful little fraternity out upon its mission. If it shall succeed in annoying some and cheering others, —many more of the latter than of the former, I trust—it will have done its duty and served its whole purpose.

While the bee is capable of stinging, it also has the instinct of honey-making. Its saccharine processes have much to do with flowers.

"THIRTEEN" AND TWELVE OTHERS.

"THIRTEEN."

"THIS will never do," cried Mrs. Mannell.

"What is wrong?" exclaimed Judge Bryan.

"There are only thirteen at the table, and I am sure I am not ready to be called home, either on earth or to glory."

"Well," said Mr. Mannell, "there is no Judas to put out, shall we call in the maid?"

"That would at least be fulfilling the scriptural injunction," urged the Rev. Barton, "to go into the by-ways and hedges and compel them to come in."

"If only Mr. Andrews had come back; the 'meountins' must have an uncommon fascination for him. But, then, we ought to have known better than to have fourteen in camp; somebody is sure to be absent from every meal."

"I move you that all the ill-luck of each day be ordered upon the absent member," said Mr. Street, who, being a retired railroad official, knew how to punish the careless.

"No, no; he will have enough bad luck in missing his rations of pork and beans," exclaimed one of the ladies.

"And you forget," said Mrs. Andrews, "that in this case I, as one of the thirteen, should be afflicted if anything befall my absent husband; so we should not escape after all."

"As this is to be an occasion of radical motions," said the Judge, taking a radish delicately between his thumb and finger, "I move that we conduct ourselves as belonging to an enlightened age, eschew old women's fables, and possess our souls in peace. Of course none of us thinks that if we thirteen sit at meat to-night, any law of nature or grace will be broken on account of the number of the company. Hence no ill can befall us from that source."

"The Judge has spoken wisely, as usual," remarked the Minister. "Nature is too large, and God too unchanging to permit any whim or accident of our little lives to alter the procession of His plans."

"Well, it looks to me just like flying into the face of Providence," whispered a pious little soul to her neighbor.

"Why not into His arms just as well?" was the reply.

"It may be true," said Mr. Merritt, "that thirteen per cent. of the race are traitors, but it does not follow that there must be a Judas in every group of thirteen."

"That's a business man's view of the matter, and quite sensible;" said Mrs. Truner, whose knowledge of affairs as well as books was rare.

"All this assumed or real fear of warnings, signs, and dreams arises from a false notion of the Deity and His government," broke in Rev. Barton. "From some source our slavish minds got the idea that God was doing a small barter business with us, taking our prayers and giving us rods in return; but, that he was kind enough to make a dead clock strike, or an owl hoot, a few hours before the calamity came, that we might have a slight forewarning for penitence. A narrow notion of God, and it has kept the concepts of men small and contracted, and will, until there is a strike for truth."

"I don't see but that these delicacies taste just as well as if there were a score here," said the Judge. "It is a matter of conscience as to our inner happiness, and a matter of physical law as to our outer comfort. I do not mean to say, ' Let us eat, drink, and be merry, for to-morrow we die ;' that is still worse than Paganism. Rather, that we should obey the ' Thou oughtest' of the Soul, and nature's laws as far as we are able. Then thirteen or thirty, the results will be the same."

"Thirteen men on a jury are sometimes vexing, are they not, Judge?"

" What do you mean, Mr. Street ? "

" I mean the twelve jurymen and the winning attorney."

"Not so vexing as when there are fourteen of us."

" Good ! the Judge has dealt with wits so long he knows how to keep his own."

" Thanks, Sir Preacher; allow me to return by saying that you often give yours away."

" You are mistaken; I draw my salary regularly, even through a summer vacation."

" Ah ! then that accounts for your not being orthodox. It is rank heresv for a preacher to receive his salary."

" A heresy for which he is not likely to be burned—unless he shouldn't spend it well."

" Keep those two gentlemen out of Hell, Mrs. Mannell."

" I will ; " refilling their glasses with ice water.

" The part of Lazarus ? "

"Come, come; the conversation is entirely too religious for me," protested Mr. Mannell, whose chief occupation was to convince country merchants that the universe swings around the jobbing house of Jewell & Company.

" I have a suggestion," quietly interrupted Mrs. McLaylin, who thought a vast deal more than she said. "Let us keep strict account, each one for himself, during our first week in the Adirondacks, and note whatever of evil or good befalls; then call an Anti-superstition convention here in Camp

Flume, one week from last night. Let that forever decide it."

"Agreed," assented all except the pious little
woman, who protested: "Let the week begin with
to-day; you forget yesterday was Friday."

"Good!" roared the gentlemen.

"I never could understand," mused the Minister,
"why any Christian should be afraid of Friday,
since it is such a significant day in his faith. It
seems to me that everything great, everything
involving human life and human love, should
begin on this crucifixion day, if days are to be
marked at all. Friday should be my wedding
day if it were to do over again. I wish I had been
born on Friday."

"Oh, dear, if I can only keep those home-sick
whip-poor-wills quiet to-night! If I don't you
must please count me out, for I just can't stand it;
something *will* happen."

"How would it do, Mrs. Fearling, to put cotton
in your ears? I suppose if you didn't hear them,
nothing could happen."

"I don't know, I'm sure."

"I want to add a suggestion to yours, Mrs.
McLaylin."

"Do so, Judge."

"It is this: that none of us permits a single
action to be governed by superstition, old or new,
during this week."

"With a forfeit if one forget?"

"Yes; everyone who is caught, or catches himself, so governed, or about to be so governed, shall pay one dollar into the summer's reading fund."

"Please leave me out," sighed Mrs. Fearling again. "It would break me up; I haven't money enough now to last until Mr. Fearling comes—if he comes at all, and I just know he won't; something will be sure to happen. He had to go back twice the day we started to the train; I wanted him to walk backwards to the house, but—"

"There's the first dollar, Mrs. Fearling."

"First dollar? From me? How do you make that out? I'm sure—"

"How could Mr. Fearling's going back affect his future conduct?"

"Why, don't you see, Judge," said Mr. Street, "a man so forgetful as that could easily forget he had a wife at all. And more than likely when Mrs. Fearling gets home, she will find her place taken by a younger and handsomer woman—if that be possible."

"You brute."

"Et tu brute?"

"Slang is worse than superstition."

"Slang? That is Latin, the best of old Roman pronunciation."

"Well, how shall we put in the day? The Judge and the Preacher will follow the shades of Walton. The ladies are going to the Flume for a little sketching and climbing, with the children."

"I don't know whether to try the rod to-day or not," replied the Judge. "I heard the cry of a loon last night, and they say trout won't bite —"

"Hold! there, my Arbiter of Justice," shouted Mr. Merritt. "A dollar, please. What a weak race we are to let these Pagan notions control us, or to listen to old women's fables! What has the cry of a loon to do with trout biting? The dollar biter is bit."

"Gentlemen, if you will be quiet a minute, I shall convince you of your error. It is not superstition. It is a scientific fact that the two phenomena are always found together."

"So, too, with the ground-hog's shadow and the late spring," said one.

"The four-leaf clover and fortune," said another.

"Horseshoes and witches," cried a third.

"And rain on Easter."

"Well, I have noticed time and again," eagerly exclaimed Mrs. Fearling, "that if it rains on Easter —"

"Ha! ha! The Judge and Mrs. Fearling are two of a kind."

"Come, Judge, fork over the fine, you are in the habit of imposing them, try paying one."

"I still insist that I am right, scientific —"

"So does Mrs. Fearling. You drink from the same fountain."

"Say no more, gentlemen; here is the dollar."

"Who shall be our treasurer? The prospects are that it will be a very responsible office."

" I move the Judge be given the office; it will be convenient for him, especially if he wishes to make himself a loan to meet the demands of the old women's fables."

" How far are we from the Canada line ? "

" If you gentlemen would read, you would know that that joke is antique since the new extradition laws. Now let us be honest in the day's record."

"Certainly, Judge, unless we should run across some scientific correlation."

" That must do, or I will pole the jury," swinging his fishing rod high above their heads.

There was little in the vicinity of Camp Flume to encourage superstition; but very much to lift the mind into a broader view of nature, and of the Absolute. It was in the midst of the beautiful Keene Valley, said to be the rarest mountain-guarded rest-spot in America. Near by are double-helmeted Giant, nearly four thousand feet above the level of the sea; Noon-Mark; Dix, rising in its splendor of five thousand feet; while to the right and far away, old Marcy, vast and consummate in its strength, toys with the inconstant clouds in stately indifference.

The Au Sable river from the south runs its pilgrimage the winding length of the maple and elm shaded valley, hurrying on to meet its bride from the Indian Pass, journeying soon together through Au Sable Chasm to the lake.

Flume Camp gets its name from an audacious little sprite of a brook, scampering down its narrow way to the river. Sometimes a hanging thread, again a little sun-shot pool, and then a loiterer, climbing by easy stages carefully down its rock-ladder, between straight stone walls a hundred feet high, covered an inch or more with moss.

A little, tiny, daring thing, braving giant rocks and forbidding caverns; singing, careless, free, wayward but winning, it never fails in obedience to its Master.

A child in Nature. A wee part of the great, stupendous whole,—the Universe,—which clashes, and dashes, and rushes, or, is dead calm to our senses; but forever and forever yielding to One, absolutely yielding, every instant.

Whether the mocking brook, or the reason which measures, admires or reproduces it in art, all is in the Process, all in the deeper Plan, of the Universal Reason.

To thoughtful minds, mountain ranges are not productive of little gods. All nature becomes only one vast kissed face under the full lips and inspiring breath of the Infinite.

No fretful cringing of nerves, no disordered functions of the body, not even deranged functions of the brain, can long take the place of reverent faith there.

2

Nature may be crystallized Evolution. Humanity has a better fate.

All is well.

The God of nature and of grace is One—the gods of clod-fashioned fancy are not at all.

What does one care. for the attic of religious rubbish, the debris of the effete ages, when he stands on Mount Marcy's Summit, in the revealing sunlight against the cobalt blue of the hill-banded horizon?

Little fears and puny dogmas snap under his feet like the century-dead pine twigs, as he climbs. Little forms of worship slip from off his soul like the moss on the damp logs, as he marches over their prostrate lengths.

Nature is great. Man, the fulfillment and further prophecy of nature is still greater. But He, the Absolute, the Source and End of both, is Greatest!

"Here comes Mr. Andrews now; we must initiate him into the new society."

"Keep quiet," said the Judge, "and let him fall into the pit."

"Oh, he is too sensible to weave any dead paganism into his thoughts."

"Thank you," rather sharply responded the Judge.

"But I wonder what's the matter. See how fast he walks. Hello, Jonathan!"

"Where's Martha?"—his wife.

"She is in the tent."

"And all right?"

"Certainly, what's wrong? You act as though you had seen a ghost."

"I came frightfully near it. I went to sleep up by the Flume while I was writing, and—talk about dreams, gentlemen! I can't say I believe in them."

"Belshazzar did," said the Judge gravely, nudging Street.

"I thought I heard my name called three times distinctly."

"That was just as we began to eat, thirteen of us. I told you something terrible would happen," soberly interrupted Mrs. Fearling.

"Hush!" whispered the Judge close at her ear.

"And then I saw Martha fall from the high cliffs just above me. I jumped to catch her, and blame me if I didn't come confounded near falling into the gorge before I could get awake. It may be superstition, friends, but I ran nearly all the way down here; I never had such a shock in my life. If there had been anything wrong with Martha, I never should have scoffed at dreamers again."

"But since there isn't anything wrong," said the Judge, eager to avenge himself, "it will cost you just one dollar. I am the treasurer, and I demand payment."

"A dollar for what?"

"For admission into the Anti-superstition Amalgamated Association, assembled for the summer at Camp Flume, Essex county, New York. "

Then the whole affair was gone over in minutia. In his glee over the hallucination of his dream, Mr. Andrews handed the treasurer a two-dollar note. "Keep the change. One payment in advance. "

The camp broke up for the day in high spirits. Soon Judge Bryan and Mr. Barton were wending their way to the nearest rapids to throw for trout.

"Isn't there danger, Barton, of carrying this business too far? See little Mrs. Fearling; already she thinks we are worse than Infidels. And are we not on the road to undermine all faith, amusing as our little contract seems ? "

"Some kinds of faith need undermining, or, rather, need showing up, that men may see that there is nothing beneath them to be mined away. One of them is this man-idea of God. An angry God, a fancy-tickled God, an impatient, quick-tempered, son-murdering, and race-damning God! I tell you, Judge, my soul revolts at the shameful turning of Hebrew poetry, child-symbols, into the religious realism of the nineteenth century. We have gone mad dogmatizing, we Protestants. It is time for a new Protestantism. It is coming. Not led by the priests this time, but by the people. We have attempted to put into human concept and speech the expressionless idea of God—His Attributes and Activities. We have dogmatized

the Son, the Holy Spirit, the Incarnation, and the
Atonement, until it is a wonder there is a worship-
er in all the world. The makers of dogmas may
have had some larger and unexpressed concepts
back of their creeds, but the masses of the people
possess only the form. The Roman Catholic idea,
originally, was to have the people see God through
images, but the untaught masses persist in seeing
God in the image. Protestantism has not done
much better until recently. Just now the cries of
the people for bread instead of stones, and above
all, the creedless Christian Endeavor movement,
are hopeful signs. It may all have been a part of
the mind's Evolution towards the true God idea."

"I think so, and we ought to be charitable."

" True, if being charitable does not also mean
being blindly contented. Did it ever strike you
as peculiar that Jesus always spoke of His Father
as Love—an emotion ? Indeed his oneness with the
Father lay chiefly in that he was the manifestation of that Love; its image, as it were. Necessarily
God is more than that. For above all real emotion
must be thought. As absolute as is God's Love
must be also his Intelligence. And when one has
thought and emotion he will unqualifiedly have
Will, action.

" The stir of the nations just now is proof, in addition to the activity of Nature for so many æons,
that God is the Absolute Personality, combining
these three elements in Infinity. There is no per-

sonality without them. What deeper personality can be conceived? Why insist, then, that God's personality goes beyond these, when it cannot? If their compound in Man is beyond comprehension, surely much more so in the Eternal. With me, these elements of myself are a matter of self-consciousness. And also, chief of all, their existence in the selfhood of God is a matter of consciousness in me, His offspring. Revelation, and design in Nature may confirm it and give it direction, they cannot prove it. Kant said truly: 'It is not certain, (or demonstrable) that there is a God, but *I know He is.*'"

"That gives me a new idea. I have long seen that the law of our land is meant to be the manifestation of the three-fold personality of the people, but I never applied it to theology. The law of God's processes in the physical realm and in mind, is the manifestation of his Personality."

"The Greeks were right. God is Immanent. Not as a blind force, but as Intellectual, Emotional and Actual Force. What a beautiful picture Jesus drew for his disciples of this great fact! 'Not a sparrow falleth;' 'Every hair of your head is numbered.' And again, when he soothed angry Galilee, loosened nature's grip from off the very body of Lazarus, and blighted with the lightning of his eye the barren fig tree."

"What, then, is the true relation of the individual to God?"

"To get his thought, emotion, and willed activity as nearly as possible into line with God's, so far as God has revealed them relative to human life."

"The incidents of nature, pain and death, are not evils to him, then, you mean?"

"That is just it. We count them evil because their issue lies out of the realm of the senses to which we are such willing slaves. They are parts of the whole plan. They come to all, and not to each one as an Independent Will may decree, but to each as his contact with his environment brings the condition of their coming. But if by prayer and worship he shall have come up to God in will, even these present ills may be averted or turned into blessings."

"What a comforting faith!"

"What a true faith. All truth is comforting. The promise of the Holy Spirit was comforting to the disciples because it should 'guide them into all truth.' What cared they for prisons or martyrdom? God was at hand."

"You believe in the miracles of Christ, then?"

"Surely. Why deny them? What is a miracle?"

"We ordinarily define it as a violation of natural law by some higher power."

"And ordinarily give both God and reason the lie. The resurrection of Christ from the dead is no more a miracle than a flash of electricity. One we see every day, it has become ordinary;

the other is not usual, but is extraordinary. We can't comprehend, much less explain either. To my mind they are both of one realm, and of one spirit, and of one movement—the one lower, the other higher—towards a common end. There can be no greater miracle than life, whether in a moss-leaf or in a risen Christ.

" We all believe in Evolution. It means passing from lower to higher forms by resident forces—the resident Infinite force, I would add. If the human condition has already attained the height of Reason, Love and Worship (since nothing is ever lost) what must be its next condition? But we also believe that phenomena are not life, that the essence of life is hidden. Even Spencer admits that the atom is a mode of the Infinite. It it were not for our physical senses there would be no universe as we now see it. If, then, true life is underneath phenomena, and is not material at all —and every great science admits it—why may not the next condition of the soul, in its evolution, be super-sensible, wholly spiritual? What more does revelation reveal than science guesses ?"

"I am charmed, my brother. Your logic is invincible, even upon scientific hypotheses; your philosophy, saving and purifying."

" But, Judge, the speckled beauties are slipping through these waters, and we shall go hence empty-handed, loon or no loon. We must desist.

But this fine air, this patient quiet, will be conducive to high thinking. And to-night we can string our thoughts. May there be as many fish on your string as thoughts."

"Thanks for your delicate compliment. There will be if you angle for me."

"There, that will do."

"A telegram for Mrs. Fearling," announced the bell boy from Flume Cottage.

"Oh dear! oh dear! it has come sooner than I expected. I knew all this wicked plotting against Providence would have some fearful end."

"Now, Mrs. Fearling," said the Minister, in whom, superstitiously, she had unbounded confidence despite his heresies, "don't worry. It may not be anything bad at all. Shall I read it for you?"

"Yes; wait till I get my camphor bottle."

The Judge wanted to add that since she had been the only one to defend the "faith," surely no calamity would come upon her.

"Come home as soon as you can. Nellie not well. No danger. D. H. F."

"Oh! my dear girl! to think I should have come away and left you at such a time! When can I start? Nellie and her husband live at Chicago, you know. Can I go to-night?"

When she was gone, a sober little spell came upon the now definitely-fixed thirteen. It look-

ed a little queer. Had misfortune already pushed open the door they had too rudely shut? Was
this the grim mocking of Fate, thus suddenly to
imprison them within the horrible condition of
just thirteen and no more, until every moment
would be lived in expectation of some horror?

Ten minutes passed without a word. Even
jocose Mr. Street was silent, and evidently far
away.

It was getting serious. Who would break the
spell?

Had they not better abandon the project after
all? Was it wise to play with the invisible?

The Judge gravely rose from his chair, and
seizing a mountain-cap started around the room.

"As treasurer of the A. A. S. A. I demand
the forfeit of one dollar each. We agreed that
if any member should be caught, or should catch
himself, being governed——"

"Enough, Judge, " said Mr. Street, "that's my
first, anyway; you are still one ahead of me."

There were twelve dollars in the cap when it
came to Mr. Barton. " We were to be honest. I
will be so. My only thought on the matter was,
that since Mrs. Fearling was the only one who
had not betrayed the 'faith,' she was not Judas;
and, therefore, though suddenly called from us,
no harm could befall her, though the whole thing
were true and not a delusion. I believe I am
free from superstition. Until I am convinced that

I am not, I cannot contribute to the funds of the society."

"Let him off, Judge. His funds are probably low, and then, since Judas is still here the suspicion will arise that perhaps Mr. Barton is he."

"Friends, I feel that we must not again, even in this innocent way, speak lightly of that most solemn night and sacred company. It is revolting to think that an irreverent church has coupled it with a senseless superstition, putting it in the mouth of every profane wretch. But we, as the guardians of the sepulchre and its associations, must teach a better lesson. Avarice, theft, treachery, will always be the black-visaged stranger, traitor, at the Lord's Communion; while trust, yearning, and crying, 'The Comforter, the Comforter!' with Peter, will always be the Lord's most pleasing friend, supping with Him. We do well to uncover the fallacy of such a superstition, but let us do it with reverent hands. I know I have not offended you."

"No, but have called us to ourselves," earnestly replied the Judge.

"Will you please come to order?" said the Judge, pounding the rough table with his fist. It was the end of the seventh day at Camp Flume.

"Do I hear a nomination for the chairman of this Association?"

"I move that the Rev. Barton, the only non-contributor to the forfeit fund, become its permanent chairman," said Mr. Merritt. When the vote had been declared, Mr. Barton took the chair with a soberness in marked contrast with the general jollity.

"I feel that we are about to institute a great movement. I have determined, through the agency of the various Young People's Societies of the church, to organize groups of thirteen all over the land, to be known as Anti-superstition Companies. Not to evangelize the world, not for charities, but for the sole purpose of ridding individual lives of the ' fear ' of God and a false notion of worship. I will not enter into details to-night. Suffice it to say, that in my judgment, it will do more to purify Romanism, Calvinism, Christian Science and Spiritualism of their false-hoods, and converge all great movements towards one absolute God, one revealing Christ, and one reverent life, than all the expositions ever written. It runs deep. It touches many great dogmas: the operation of the Holy Spirit, Conversion, Prayer, the Devil, and even Hell itself. But to the purpose of the evening. First we shall listen to the report of the treasurer."

The Judge soberly arose, and adjusting his spectacles, proceeded to read in deep chest-tones : "Mr. Street, two fines. One for self-confessed alarm over Mrs. Fearling's telegram, the other for a remark concerning a red-headed girl and a white horse."

"I give notice here of protest against the second item," shouted Mr. Street, "on the ground of its being irrelevant, immaterial and irreligious."

Mr. Street was called down by the chairman: "The treasurer will proceed without further interruption."

"Mrs. Truner, three fines. One for telegram, another for an incautious remark about spilled salt, and the third for asking the treasurer to make a wish over the new moon. Mrs. Mannell, one for telegram, the other for moving away from a 'death-tick' in the west door-post of Camp Flume."

But we need not follow the list of fines further. They were nearly all of a humorous nature, closing with the Judge's three, the loon, the telegram, and a proposed "philopena" with Mrs. Merritt. There were thirty-six dollars in the treasury. Twenty would be sufficient for the summer reading supply. It was voted to hand over the remainder to the chairman as a correspondence fund in the organization of the new order.

Following are a few of the reports of the week's good and ill luck:

Mr. Street's: "Haven't missed a meal."

"That has been our misfortune," cried several.

"Have climbed to the top of the Giant without

a guide and returned alive. Have a deer's head,
as you all know, mounted ready for shipment
home."

"He bought it at the 'Adirondack House'
for seventeen dollars," whispered the Judge to
Mrs. Truner.

"Have just had a letter from Charley, saying
the house had finished a deal netting ten thousand dollars. Heard of a bear that was caught
several miles away from here last winter. Traced
the story and found, first, it had only left one
foot in the trap; and last, that the foot belonged
to a cat of the pole persuasion. No, I didn't buy
the trap. Havn't had a single mosquito bite. Conscience has been clear, and, best of all, every mail
brings me word of the health and content of my
babies at home—God bless them."

Mrs. Truner's report: "The pain in my head
is gone. I have lived more in seven days in
these mountains than in seven years before."

"That makes you six years my senior, doesn't
it, dear?" said her husband. A look silenced him.

"I never knew how near one could get to
Heaven, and how much one could love friends until now. It has been a sweet, tender, dream-like
week to me. If thirteen had nothing to do with
it, twelve of you had, I know."

"Count God," exclaimed Mr. Barton.

"I have, and as I never did before. If thirteen has affected me at all, it has been in the

thought that, after all, when Judas repented, and threw down the accursed silver, he may have been forgiven by his Master and the number thus kept unbroken, a symbol of God's mercy rather than a mark of fear to little souls."

" I have long believed that, Mrs. Truner," again exclaimed the Minister.

" I have written a little verse out of the fullness of my joy. I ask to have it made a part of my report :

> "Thy tears, oh son of perdition, may later quench
> The fires of thy soul-losing love of place and pelf.
> His blood may redder be than all thy scarlet sin,
> His mercy deeper than thy hateful, traitrous self."

A solemn hush had come upon all from the experience of this true woman.

The Judge followed. " Camp Flume will long be held sacred in my memory.' For some time—and this is my confession—I have been hanging between my old, blind faith and atheism. Strange that, a teacher of discrimination in law, I had never learned it in religion. My mind .turned away from the idea of the absolute sovereignty of Deity and the slavery of man. An avenging God, taking his pleasure in over-riding weak mortals upon whom the sin-taint of centuries had come, leaving them all broken and helpless, was the nightmare of my religious musings. My own consciousness told me that God is, and that the soul is of Him, and immortal; and that the struggle after righteousness can be the only bond between God and man. But I failed to discern between my superstition and my rational faith. I came near giving intuition and reason the lie, denying myself, and crying out ' There is no God.' Nothing at times but the haunting voice of my youth, saying, ' The fool hath said in his heart, There is no God,' kept me in my pride from this open denial. Prayer only mocked me. I had been taught to pray for physical blessings as though they depended upon my praying. I now know that prayer is a spiritual petitioning for spiritual blessing, and has its answer not merely in the changed mood of the petitioner, but in an actual answering with spiritual strength and consolation from the Great Heart. I never was more grateful than now, however, for physical blessings, for existence in a physical condition where law is so unchanging, and bounty so unfailing, that individual effort can secure daily bread ; gratitude make it doubly sweet.

" I never understood Revelation. I know now that God and immortality are in all human consciousness ; that revelation comes, not as a mystifier, but as a revealer of particular ends to be reached by particular means. The Bible has ten-fold more meaning to me now than it did. Authorship, incidents and methods of inspiration, have no relative value compared with the Christo-centric prophesy in the old, and fulfillment in the new

Covenant. The Trinity as a psychological problem maddened me into sullenness at times. Now, I apprehend the one God, Eternal, Everlasting; Jesus his special exponent in the flesh, now become King of kings, and Lord of lords; and the Holy Spirit the personified process of the Father's saving activities. I am surprised to find how clearly Jesus taught that the Holy Spirit's work should be hidden from the senses of men, his testimony to be made through chosen human agents by mouth and pen.

"The whole field of Eschatology seems clear to me now. Sin is the violation of known law. No guilt attaches otherwise. There is one life, here and hereafter. But where there is irresponsible ignorance here, light will be given hereafter.

To *know* God is to *love* men in the sacrificial spirit of Jesus Christ. I believe, therefore, the Sermon on the Mount to be real, whereas I once thought it merely ideal, figurative. I am convinced that the ' meek shall inherit the earth.'

"I feel as though I had been the betrayer, but am at last willing to confess my faith, even before the priests, before whom I am resolved to fling the purchase price of my denying kiss. Even this thirteen of Camp Flume shall have no Judas but a repentant one."

As this great man talked, the place seemed like the Camp of Israel with the flaming Shekinah. Fine in physique, noble of brow, strong in mental

3

power, magnetic, full of great impulses, renowned
on the bench for his justice, stern in his denunciation of the violation of law; it is not surprising
that the little company felt in the presence of a
master, who had become as a little child. His
voice was tremulous, not with any maudlin senti-
ment, nor by overwrought nerves, but with an
emotion of worship, and a mental grasp of great
and high truths. He had traveled a long way
in seven days toward the very heart of the
Mighty; and while it made him eloquent as
Paul, he had also become as tender as Mary.
No Damascus light had called him to Apostleship,
but the light that lighteth every man which
cometh into the world had been shining through
the shadows of his life all the week. As children
lean against their mother's knees, while she talks
of angels and of the Bethlehem cradle, so these
listened and watched, dim-eyed. They caught,
every one, some large measure of his spirit. The
mood divine was upon all. No little physical or
hysterical thrills were moving within them. No
boisterous manifestation without. They had seen,
often with disgust, the hypnotic influence of religious excitement; but now they were the witnesses
of the power of the truth over mind. Gospel truth,
Holy Spirit-quickened truth. They remembered
how on Pentecost the *spoken words* of Peter convinced and converted; how Paul preached to
Lydia, and Philip opened his mouth to the Ethio-

pian's conversion. Always and everywhere men
have been truly converted only through the *truth*
put into the form of their mental conception.

" *The truth shall make you free.*"

"Now, Mr. Barton," suggested some one, quietly.

" You have just had my report. Everything
else of the week is lost to me in that. I was never
so sure of God, so sure of revelation, so sure of
Eternal Mercy and Life as now. It has been a
blessed week, an upper-chamber company. Our
Lord and Master has not been far away.",

All was silence for many minutes. The cool
air of the mountain summits came softly down its
pine-fragrant way, soothing away doubt as a
mother's evening song, but astir with the breath
of God.

Away to the southwest, serene Hurricane leaned
against the star-flecked sky in repose, and with
an uplift of stature like one who, feeling his secu-
rity, stands poised between great dangers, confi-
dent of the issue. The lonely whip-poor-will told
his tale of faithful watch-care; in it was no dismal
note of death-warning to these exalted souls thinking now of home, of burdens laid aside for this
brief rest.

Down the valley the northern lights were moving
in splendid panorama from east to west. Their
uplifted arms gave one the thought that somewhere a mighty chorus of voices was chanting
Nature's vespers. From the cottage near by a

clear, soprano strain grew upon them by swelling measures, until it awakened within them echoes of some far-off, half-lost music of other years. Sweeter, but stronger, it came: "Hope thou in God."

Faint, delicate echoes came up from the brook-riven flume below, like the accompaniment of unseen singers. The spell could not be broken; they would not break it for golden wealth. The heavenly portals were ajar. The earth-soul was in tune with the Over-Soul. Their quiet rapture and deepening resolution were a prayer, an all-controlling prayer. In his wordless heart of hearts, Mr. Barton was communing in marvelous nearness with the Mountain Preacher of Judea. If words could express his emotion they would be: "Dear, wounded, despised, pierced Man of Sorrow; Lover of wounded, despised, pierced men of griefs; Walker of crested waves, and Healer of sick souls; Thou earth-held Son of the Infinite Love, Thou constant, tenderest, Only Brother of my infirm and inconstant self; by Thy Spirit, by Thy truth, Thyself lead me to think only God, to feel only God, to will only God. Thus let the Highest dwell in me, until that great day when I shall dwell with Thee forever and forever. Through me, come Thou, O Christ, into other helpless souls, until the brotherhood of man shall be truly begun. Amen and Amen."

The Judge was the first to break the silence.

"How I wish Mrs. Fearling might be here to-night. I believe this reverent spirit would seem infinitely better to her than her small religious fears ; her quakings and unrest."

"A telegram for the chairman of the A. Anti-superstition Association. Charges paid," came the shrill voice of the bell-boy, startling them half out of their wits.

"What in the world can that mean?"

"Who knows of our existence?"

"Or our whereabouts?" came from several voices.

"Read it quick!"

"Give it to Mr. Barton."

"Nellie is the mother of fine twin boys. All doing well. I am a convert. Will send two dollars for the forfeit-fund by next mail.—GRAND-MA."

THE FAIRIES AT AU SABLE CHASM.

"The Lodge" was locked. It was dead of night. But Au Sable Chasm was countlessly thronged. For the first time gay laughter could be heard above the roar of the channel-plunged torrent.

The moon for some time had been gleaming down upon the long and sinuous water-flow winding along like some angry monster between straight rock-walls, lifting sheer two hundred feet their inlaid columns of inexpressible beauty. On this particular night her path would long lie just overhead, and the fairies might dare the darkness of the chasm without risk to their supple limbs.

For many seasons they had heard of the wonders of Au Sable. Boastful little sprites on Mount Marcy and old White Face, and even the contented little elves, centuries old, on Lake Placid, had been vexed again and again as they overheard thoughtless visitors extol the charms of the gardened-Gorge miles away.

For days past tiny runners had been leaping from rock to rock, swinging from pine to pine, swimming brooks and lakes, until the news had gone like forest fire: "A midnight meet at Au Sable."

From Marcy to Avalanche, from McIntyre to Seward across the Indian Pass, from Placid and the Saranacs down to Hurricane, from Keene and Pleasant Valleys, the energetic and thoroughly excited little kings and their entire kingdoms were prepared for flight, when the signal should burn on Marcy's heights.

The Adirondacks were never so astir. It was rumored that on *this* night the signal flames would fly. The birds, frightened-eyed, were hushed all day. Little children danced back and forth to their mammas with the strangest puzzling questions. Even papas nodded at their pole's end, and dreamed queer dreams of streams where the trout always bite.

Not a soul slept in all the Range when night came on. Some said there was too much electricity in the air, and that it would storm before morning. Others danced like mad on the polished floors of the great hotels. The babies kept their wide-awake nurses running from parlor to parlor for numberless good-night kisses from bright-eyed mammas.

Just as the clock struck twelve every papa and mamma yawned and lazily sought their beds, while the sweet babies turned their faces to the wall and slept sound and dreamless. The flames on Marcy had kissed the moonbeams just at twelve with gay little quirks of half-strange embarrassment.

Like a rising, sun-smitten mist the invisible populace of the Adirondacks from lake and mountain swept up, and converged Eastward. Soon vast Lake Champlain was seen asleep under the watching thousand-eyed sky. It stirred gently in faint ripples, like a babe smiling in its dreams, as it felt the thrill of the oncoming host of fairies.

Swooping down at last, and settling in serried ranks on poised wings, they hovered just below the "Rainbow Falls," near the entrance of Au Sable Chasm.

Thousands of human eyes have beamed with the reflection of the tinted bows in the spray, seen here in the bright sunlight. But never before had moon-and-star-beam rainbows been seen by the sharpest eyes. There they hung, ten thousand times ten thousand, crossing and recrossing in countless curves set in inimitable geometric designs. The whir of wings after a moment's silence was finely expressive of their pleased astonishment.

Suddenly the after-silence was broken by a sonorous, rotund voice calling above the waters. At once they knew it to be their great Priest and Prophet, who had been foremost in their new venture upon undiscovered territory. They turned with fixed attention, as was their wont when their religious teacher spoke.

He stood on the loftiest pinnacle of "Pulpit Rock," just at the bend of the Gorge as one goes down. A huge pile of layered granite overhangs the foam here—a fit place for elemental nature's Priest to interpret her laws if He would.

But the power of the night and the scene were upon this elfin prophet. He spoke of light and truth; that his people were Nature's highest expression. He declared that music and pictures and motion were personified in them. They must make no discords, nor group into any ugly forms, nor move out upon any unlighted lines. So what had threatened to be a frenzied assault and seizure, suddenly turned to an altar hour and worship.

A chant followed. I wish you might have heard it. All the songs of the birds, all the hum of the bees, all the murmur of waters, and the sighing of winds were in it. Yes, and at its close, all the thunder and swell of all the torrents, in all the gorges, as it swung up and up to the stars, and to the Fashioner of stars !

Then slowly and reverently they began their descent into the Chasm. Clinging to jutting ledges, clasping bending ferns, drinking dew from the thousand blue-bells, regardless of the iron rail and path, they came to the very water's edge.

They stood in astonishment before the "Elephant's Head," projecting from huge "Spit Rock." The Gothic Mountain people declared that it belonged to the "Elephant's Body" of their mountain, so plainly seen from Lake Placid, and began to talk of gigantic schemes for its immediate removal. "The head and body must be put together."

Still others gasped with delight in the dashing spray, plunging back and forth in a whirlpool of waters.

Many scanned the rocks for sign-boards to catch the human idea of this unsurpassed beauty. As they turned to the left they read: "Devil's Oven," and "Hell Gate." They groaned with indignation that anything so sublime should be coupled with such repulsive and horrible notions. Their religion was chiefly of heaven anyway. They had heaven already, they said. Why think of hell? They hated the Devil. They wanted nothing whatever to do with him.

They instantly changed these offensive names to "Elves' Cave," and "Moonbeam Pass," for just then the moon hung directly over their heads so that there was scarcely a shadow in the Gorge save at the sharp corners here and there. But when, leaping on, they saw "Jacob's Ladder" rising straight and inviting out of the very water up to the stars, step by step, their exultation knew no bounds. They leaped across, they bounded up to its very heights, singing their hallelujahs from its moon-lit summit.

Others kept on, walking on tiny rock-ways where not even birds dared to perch.

The hallelujah chorus from the top of Jacob's Ladder sent down showers of maple leaves upon the now quieter waters. They were seized eagerly and made to serve as boats, guided with unerring skill. As the elves leaned over the boat-edges they looked down into forty feet of dark, shadowy water. But shot with moonbeams as it was, their keen eyes saw to the very bottom, where lay a wealth of stones, both as to color and form never equaled in their most secret brooks on Marcy and Hurricane.

Ten, twenty, and thirty feet apart, the great colored walls rose until the sky seemed to rest upon them. Seamed and rent and notched at the curves like great wheels, now moss-covered, now bare and smooth like marble, now hung with ferns, and plants growing with flower-cups down, they were veritable hanging gardens.

The elves did well to re-name the Gorge "Heaven's Shorter Path."

Above the clatter they heard once more the prophet's voice. They hastened on, expecting another surprise. Poised above one another's heads until they formed a hollow dome, looking down they saw the wonderful "Jacob's Well." Into a little plateau of hard rock some water-spun stone had ground out through the years when the waters were higher than now, a resting place of

concentric circles. It had rest, doubtless, only
when it was worn out. As the result, a perfect
stone well had been sunk thirty feet or more. Inside it looked as though hugh stone rings had
been laid one upon another.

With solemn tone the prophet told them of
Jacob and the Egypt of the Sun-elves, until they
hung listening with bated breath.

Suddenly a belated firefly flashed in the great
side-depths of "Hyde's Cave," just across from
"Jacob's Well." Ten thousand sprites started
for its double entrance cut a hundred feet high.
They rolled round pebbles down the steep incline
and set the water quivering, tipping the tiny boats
from side to side. It was marvelous how these
boatmen shot the fiercest rapids with their bending leaves. Whirled about and under, they came
out only the fresher for their warm bath.

"Hide's Cave" they re-named "Lovers' Confes-
sional." Here, they said, lovers must separate at
the entrace, go within, and commune alone; then
return, meet again, and confess every desire.

Returning to the opposite side they came suddenly upon "Smuggler's Pass." They shivered and
passed quickly by, but paused and appointed a
committee of one hundred to return, explore and
re-name. Observing so many notched, wheel-like
stones on either side of the defile, they reported
"the Cave of the Mills." It was accepted.

In a moment they were at the "Post Office"—an

overhanging, narrow room, cut into a hundred cell-
like boxes for honeyed letters. Instantly every elf
fell to writing on blades of grass and flower
leaves with colored bits of sand. Such mirth, such
rallying of contending parties over a race for the
largest number of letters! Such comparing of
notes and whispered "quizzes" as made the Gorge
echo from "Pulpit" to "Table Rock.!"

Soon "Table Rock" was reached and proved a
delightful resting place. Just back of and beyond it lay the "Anvil," beneath whose shelter
a little booth had been built where "views" and
"soda pop" were sold to visitors at "reduced
rates." They did not need the views. Ten thousand negatives had already been impressed upon
a thousand tiny kodaks' film.

But the "pop!" The little elves from the
Lakes knew the pop of corks and fizz of foam well
enough to look very wise. But how to get at it was
the question. As the first bottle of "strawberry"
lay on the bar it looked like a hugh cannon load-
ed and primed. A brave little Avalanche king
suggested that they fasten the wire to a nail and
then pry the bottle up until it should slip out and
let the cork fly. In a minute all was in readiness.
Hundreds gathered about to see the fun and to
cheer their hard-working little brothers. The bottle
had been severely shaken in the melee. When at
last it slipped its wire, out came the cork with a
thunderous report, knocking a hundred little men

backward into the water, and sending the foaming pop over ten times as many more. Then there were cries of distress and fright, and shouts of laughter and derision. A few were silent. They were pouring the remainder of the contents into bluebell cups, and with little gurgles of delight letting the red juice run down their dry throats.

Even fairies learn by experience. So bottle after bottle was opened with the muzzle of the cannon pointed towards the opposite shore. When the empty bottles had been replaced in the ice-chest they called for a dance upon the broad rock.

Behind the " Anvil " rose " Sentinel " and " Cathedral Rocks "—rounded columns straight from water-edged base to tree-pinnacled point. In the spaces between these they arranged the orchestra. Tier above tier they sat, noisy, nervous, tuning, turning their music to catch the moonlight. They soon were swaying with the baton of the leader, who stood bold and commanding on the top of the " Anvil."

One had but to listen to know where Mozart, Schumann and Chopin fonnd their themes. In dreams the fairies had been their masters. But a dream's interpretation is never all the dream was.

The half-crying, half-slumbering waltz; the bright, wakeful schottische, and the great, four-square, solemn, stately march, sung their senses away. In a dreamy maze of emotion they celebrated the finding of so marvelous a Palace.

For already, as by one thought, it had been determined to transfer the Supreme Throne from Marcy to Au Sable. It needed now but the decree of the Grand Council, and the sanction and blessing of the Prophet Priest.

They stood looking off from the edge of " Table Rock," wondering what lay beyond, but too exhausted by the dance to climb further the rough paths, while a ventursome little elf, exploring an under-rock path, discovered the great boat which has carried so many awe-spelled travelers down the Gorge, shooting fretful rapids and plunging over great wave-swells. But one word was needed. The boat was instantly filled, hundreds clinging to its sides.

I do not know what unseen guide kept them off the rocks as they dashed madly on. We know so little at best of life and its forces. But harmlessly Nature led them through. They live so close to her, she may be kinder to them than to us. I know that neither lightning, nor flood, nor wind has ever hurt one of them, while fire is their panacea for all pain. Whereas, by our rebellion against nature, we are torn and bruised and killed, they live on unscathed. Perchance when the millennial age shall come, and the New Jerusalem shall be let down out of heaven, our spiritual bodies may realize this old earth spiritualized—a Paradise Regained.

After the half-mile ride, over depths of water

sixty feet, the cliffs growing lower, they landed
at last on a level plateau. With a shout and a
scramble they turned back over the hills until
they came to the great "Stairway," with its
foot at "Table Rock." Descending, they re-
assembled with one accord about the Highest,
as they name their Supreme Monarch.

The council had held its session here in their
absence. The decree was ready. These were
the words: "By decree of the Grand Council of
the elves of the Adirondacks we proclaim these
words, signed by the light of Serius and sealed with the blood of the Hidden Altar. This
riven hill, with its living fountain, shall be and is
forever henceforth the sacred and inviolable dwelling place of the Highest and His Court. Here pe-
titions shall be heard. Here justice declared and
mercy counseled. If there be strife between two,
here it shall melt into warm embrace. If black-
ness of mind, here shall be recreative light. If the
death-touch—which comes only when one wishes
for what another has—here, under due penitence,
it shall be removed. Every elf an elf, no more,
no less. Rulers and ruled alike. We rule for
Elfdom, you serve for Elfdom. One end—the
happiness of all. It is done."

The Priest and Prophet standing on the crown
of "Cathedral Rock," two hundred feet above
them, enrapt in a soft but glowing light that seemed to come from some single star (I wish I knew

which one ; I should surely tell you), with uplifted
hands, seen by every eye and heard by every ear,
catching the exact pitch of the falling waters, in
musical cadences atune with the night and the
place, breathed down upon them his Amen and
Amen.

And thus the empty, unhallowed, Au Sable
Chasm, beautiful but soulless, came to be possessed of the very heart of life.

And now every fern, every moss-leaf, every
fleck of spray, and every shadowy deep, the whole
length and depth of Au Sable is instinct with life
—the breathing, pulsing, communing Soul of the
Adirondacks.

4

MAIDEN ROCK.

THE point, as well as the place, of attack was Maiden Rock. He had been premeditating it all day. He did not want to seem abrupt, but in his present mood nothing seemed precipitous.

She had been like flint to all his sparks thus far. He wondered if there were any tinder about her.

He must speak some time. The sooner—well, it *might* be for better, it *might* be for worse; he hoped it would be for both.

Surely if scenic properties could add anything to his cause, the present moment could not be surpassed. Below them one hundred and thirty feet lay Bouquet River. Just beyond, the famous "Split Rock Falls" began its descent of one hundred feet, down its rock-rough gorge channel.

On the edge of this very rock where they stood, Eutoka, a jealousy-mad Indian maiden, years ago, restless over her lover's unkept promise to tryst with her at this romantic spot, had leaped dumb and resolute into the shallow waters below. Surely nature and romance were with him—but Fate? Well, a word, and Fate would be with

him, too; but what? It was the uncertainty of
the issue that made him hesitate.

The "Hermit Guide" who presides over the
destinies of those who visit his Gorge, had shrewdly
stepped aside after relating the legend of the rock.
A confirmed old bachelor of nearly forty winters—
summers would be better, since everything in the
Adirondacks is counted by summers—yet he had
not forgotten how much more some minutes are to
some people than to others. He had at once
guessed the secret of the young man. He was not
so sure that the sweet-faced young girl had a
secret yet.

"What an odd genius the guide is."

The silence was too oppressive; after waiting
several minutes she had decided to break it herself. Merlin Hall, her lover, had been afraid to
open his mouth for fear the first word would be
some kind of a blunder. This was a happy relief
for the moment. It gave him a decision, too. He
would wait now until Fate gave him a hint. He
would not hazard everything at a single venture.

He replied rather sarcastically: "If you have
reference to his dress and manner, I should say,
yes."

"But I don't. The idea of his building that
rustic pavilion back there in the woods. Why, it
is a perfect piece of art. Did you notice his
peculiar eyes?"

"No; I noticed the peculiar cut of his hair. There wasn't any cut."

"Oh, didn't you see anything good about him? I should have thought his playing 'Home, Sweet Home,' on the one string of his old violin would have impressed you."

"Yes, that was rather a remarkable feat. You noticed probably that he used his feet somewhat in playing it."

"Oh, well, that is because he plays so much for balls. You know he said that was his recreation."

"Yes, I should imagine that if he danced it would be recreation, an all-four, bear-fashion recreation."

"Come, you are getting positively gross."

"Well, who wouldn't? Here in the face of this white, tumbling water, and these jagged rocks, yes, and perhaps in the presence of the unhappy Eutoka, wooed, as it were, by nature, you can talk of nothing but the guide."

"Well, let us change the subject then. Shall I talk about—about—"

"Me. Talk about me. Can't you see, Bessie, what must be so plainly before your eyes? I—I fancy everyone else notices it, if you do not. Even the guide has left us in the middle of his story. I can forgive all his sins for that one righteous act."

He had not waited very long for a "leading

from Fate." Nor did he begin it himself very
gracefully. But he was an impetuous youth,
abounding in energy. He could never wait. He
had been born early in the sixties and was full
of that unspent bravery, and yearning desire for
action, which the mothers felt so keenly in the
long war days, when the fathers of even tiny babes
were on the distant field. Merlin liked nothing
better than leaping from rock to rock across some
dangerous mountain stream. He boasted that he
never fished, but preferred to hunt. He loved the
rush and noise of the chase and shot, but could not
endure the quiet of the ducking cork, even though
a speckled beauty were a possibility at the other
end of the line. He declared there was sure to be
one at the dry-end of it—mosquitoes were his *bete-
noirs*.

Something of the heroism of this war spirit was
in his wooing just now. To wait quietly he could
not, no matter how often he might resolve upon it.
Better, like Eutoka, leap and have it done with,
than climb the hills and boat the lakes in endless
suspense.

To say that Bessie looked surprised would certainly not be extravagant. Girlish in her innocence, though well-bred and cultivated, not only
in the fine arts, but having a fairly liberal education as well, she had had no dreams as yet of love—
by day. She had liked Merlin, since they had
met three weeks before on the steamer from West

Port to Plattsburg by the charity of a common
friend who knew they had chosen the same route
for the summer. Bessie was with her brother, just
from Harvard, and a little older than herself.
Merlin was alone, resting up from his first long
season in the law, in which, by this same war
spirit, he had been phenomenally successful,
having tried and gained his first case in the Supreme Court of Iowa against great legal odds.
The Iowa State Recorder had spoken of him as " one
of the most audaciously promising young men at
the Iowa bar."

Bessie had liked him because he could tell her
something of everything they saw; he was exceedingly entertaining, particularly in repartee; and,
best of all, was a lover and a student of good
books.

Their very first conversation had plunged into
American literature. They had talked of Aldrich,
Stedman, and Gilder until the twilight chill drove
them from the upper deck. By some good fortune
they had both been reading Gilder's best volume of
poems, The Celestial Fire, and were both fascinated
by its perfect mechanism and pure-souled themes.
Merlin confirmed her faith in Gilder's integrity by
telling her of his acceptance of a story for The
Century, and the payment of a large sum for it,
but its subsequent return to the author on account
of a semi-Mexican *abandon* on the part of the
hero, which at first had not struck the editor as

being so objectionable as upon a second reading. It afterwards appeared in another leading magazine. There were presumably two checks.

She startled him at the close of the conversation, as they arose, by referring to The Century as the simultaneous prophecy and fulfillment of this century of American literature and art. He had not given her credit for so great discernment. His respect for her increased from that moment. By easy stages their friendship grew until with her it had come to be a persistent belief in his honorableness, a recreative delight in his accomplishments, and a sisterly desire to be with him just for the rest it gave her. Her analysis went no further. With him, for a whole week now, friendship had been love. Half concealed, lest it should drive her from him, half revealed, because he was truthful by nature.

She turned toward him with startled eyes, her innocent, not coquettish face, begging for an explanation, with just a first consciousness beginning to bloom on either cheek. His pleading eyes needed no words to help him in their message. But they would come.

"Don't look so frightened, Bessie. You make me think of a snared bird. Nothing shall hurt you. There isn't anything threatening but,— but my love. It—it threatens nothing but your alarm, Bessie. Don't be frightened. I thought I felt small and powerless before these awful hills,

but I feel helpless as a child before your sweet
face. You could strike me down if you would,
not I, you. But you won't, Bessie? You will let
me live? Your sweet, tender eyes will lose their
scared look by and by, won't they? Just one
dimpled smile. Have they all flown? Oh, I love
you. Even nature cannot love the brooding spirit
of its Creator more. Bessie, speak to me."

"I can't," she gasped. "I can't. I—don't know
what to say. I never dreamed you—you—"

"Loved you, loved you, Bessie? What a good
word it is, when you say it right out loud. 'I love
you.' Won't you try it, Bessie?"

"I can't; I must not now. I don't know what—
oh, I must go back."

"Alone?"

"No."

"But you remember Eutoka," he replied, laughingly, to relieve her from her distress. He felt
there could be but one answer finally. At last he
was content to wait. But was it waiting? Did he
not know already? He thought he did. But she
was so shy all the way as they walked that he
scarcely dared take her hand to help her over the
slippery rocks.

Like a deer frightened at a gunshot, she was all
a-quiver lest she should hear it again. He talked
of the trail, for they soon lost it; of the absent
guide, willing now in his new mood to concede to
him all the virtues. He did possess a variety of

them. Observing he was also communicative; uncultivated, yet a gentleman; a wayfarer, yet a lover of his mountain home.

Merlin plucked every flower he could see as they crossed tiny brooks and their little blossoming valleys, and gave them to her with their homely names. He seemed possessed of a kind of frenzy. Just as when a boy, he had offended his little sister, and had offered her every coveted toy to win her back before she cried, so now he had a similar but more intense thought. "See these tiny little dots, Bessie, little drops of gold from the stars. And here," as a fancy for yellow caught him, " are the sweetest of all, the dear old buttercups, fresh as the morning dew; they never grow old. Ah, now I have a trinity of yellow for you, Bessie ; this bold Johnswort complements the modest dots and cups. Won't you take them?"

She took them mechanically, avoiding the touch of his hand, with scarcely a word. She clutched them tightly, however, as she stooped and turned to keep in the path he made for her through the bending pines.

"Now I shall gather a trinity of white." He might easily have doubled his trinity of yellow, with golden-rod, yellow daisies, and the wild hops. "Here, first of all, is the beautiful 'partridge berry.' I think I should have named it 'dove berry.' Come, see it, Bessie." He fell upon his knees, seeking the little white wax cups, the long stem of each corolla turning into soft fur, delicate and fairy-like beyond description, in its wealth of round, dark green leaves. But Bessie stood straight and still before him. He could only hope she was watching him. He dared not look up. "See, here is its red berry on this stem," and he held the bright crimson berry, not larger than a ripe currant, towards her. He felt her take both the flower and the berry more gently than before. But when he arose, she turned away.

"These white daisies I picked over by the Maiden-Rock, now if I can find one more white flower—here it is now,—this wild buckwheat, with its tiny lily-of-the-valley bloom." He might have added "deerweed," "yarrow," and the "bride's flower" to his trio of white.

"White and yellow, these shall be my colors on the field of glory. White for brotherly love to men, yellow for honor. I shall wear them for my Queen Bess."

Just then they came into a little open space, under the half shadows of the lighter branches. She seemed so alone, so distressed and far away, that he felt he must fall upon his knees, and pray back her dim eyes and dull ears. They seemed to see only beyond the pines, and to hear only the roar of the now distant falls. His soul went out to her with mighty power. He must bring her back to him.

Who can tell what psychological forces were at

play. For as he looked upon her averted face
she turned slowly toward him with a gentle lifting
of her hand, but his yearning, intense look drove
her back more securely than ever into herself.

She started on ahead. With blinding tears of
mortification and alarm he followed, reaching for
her arm in his frenzy, but an escaped branch of
spruce struck him full in the face, making his
eyes smart for a moment with intense pain. He
stood an instant pressing them with his handkerchief. Then he thought that if she could be
alone for awhile, it might serve to recover her
from the strange condition his declaration had
brought upon her.

"Bessie, where are you?" he said gently, after
an interval, tremulous with his violent heart-beat-
ings. No reply. "Bessie!" a little louder. "I
wonder if the poor child is crying? Why couldn't
I have waited? I must do something for her, if it
is only to go after the guide and leave her with
him awhile. Perhaps he can soothe her."

He peered through the understructure of the
woods, but there was no sign of her. Calling quite
loud, getting no answer but a faint echo of his own
voice, like the sweet, mocking witchery of some
playful child, he grew very uneasy. He hurried
this way and that, shouting at every turn. Per-
plexed and undecided, he sat down helplessly upon
a broken pine.

A half hour had probably passed, it seemed

endless to him, when the guide came upon him, attracted by his shouts. He told him his story. It brought out all the good in his straight, lank, unkempt nature. He seemed to know, without being told, just what the difficulty was. Some faint memory of his own youth, long in perspective, may have been quickened. He suggested the trail; that they search in both directions, before an alarm be raised.

The trail was soon found. For some reason unaccountable to himself Merlin chose the way back to Maiden-Rock. A short but difficult climb brought him within sight of it. There at its very edge sat Bessie, sobbing and swaying as if in terror. Merlin was speechless with fear. He dared not say a word lest the shock cause her to lose her balance and slip to the awful grave below. There was but one thing to do. The roar of the water would cover his footfalls. He would creep stealthily to her, and seizing her in his arms, bear her back before she could resist.

His only thought was that some sudden dementia had taken her, and that her life must be saved at any cost. He was soon just behind her, his breath coming fast and in gasps—surely she would hear his heart beat. She was talking to herself in little moans. "I do—I do love him, and I've hurt him so. I wouldn't even look at him. What shall I do?" In a moment, she never knew just how, she was standing back on the rocks with two strong arms about her.

"Forgive me, Bessie, won't you? I forgot you were just a little girl. And I love you so much. I couldn't wait to tell you."

He knew what it all meant now. He remembered by her own story, and by her anxious, tender, half-puzzled distress over her brother's reckless speech and manner, that she was just as innocent of the world's rougher thought as it is possible to be and live anywhere in this loose century. By wise mother-care, by a mind kept full of great and good things, by not a prudish, but a sweet, womanly horror of "daring," she had grown through these eighteen years utterly without guile. No half-aroused affection to be blunted by jest, and a mockery of love, had been hers. No evil realism either in life or fiction had ever painted black pictures for her secret musings. Simply a whole-souled, capable, healthy young woman kept inviolate for one love, one heart, one life. The hollow mockery of flattery had never taught her to dissemble. She had never been "coached" by her mother upon how to develop and receive declarations of love.

To her, love was some inner manifestation of the divine nature. She believed it always brought woman to her best. A woman's love should be a transparent crystal in the simplicity of its passion, but flushed with an inner flame, like some fine ruby. To her, love contained all the secrets of the primal morn of creation, all the poetry of hope, and all the permanence of a vital faith.

Moreover, in it were all the issues of her own individuality. On one side it seemed to her like the cloud and fiery pillar to the Egyptians, as it threateningly lay between the avenging pursuers and the sea-bound Israelites, dark and terrible. Then she shivered and fled. On the reverse side she saw it as the Hebrews saw, full of the glory of the Eternal.

No insinuating touch had ever set her heart fluttering with desires she could not understand. No subtly-couched words had ever started currents of thought fanning into flame misguided fancies. A woman in letters and in reason, she had known nothing more than her babyhood love until an hour ago. Even her regard for Merlin until the moment of his impulsive declaration had been in keeping with her whole life before.

But now it seemed as though she had been all this while ascending a steep hillside with its half-hidden trail, vine-walled and moss-carpeted, until this very moment she had stepped out upon a great, jutting ledge, commanding the curves of a bounteous valley, and the circuit of innumerable hills. So had her life widened, deepened, lifted within an hour.

It came when in his yearning eyes she saw herself. Such strange emotions; such fears, and yet such longings. Her heart beat so fast she could only gasp. She was beside herself for the moment. So new, so strange, so delightful, so absorbing, so alarming, she felt like a new creature in a new world. As she confessed, standing on the rock that evening: "It seemed that I could hear that poor Indian girl all the while calling me, and that I must come back to this rock. Something, I could not understand what, guided me here. I felt strong when I stood here for a moment, until I thought of you back there alone and hunting for me; then I almost fainted with the pain of it, until I felt about me some thrillingly strong force, like some great, free spirit, buoyant as fine air and cheering as wine. I felt then that nothing could harm me. I went with perfect calm to the edge of the rock and sat down. But by and by the wail of the water came up like a half-stifled sob from the rocks, and then I seemed to go all to pieces, as it were, calling for you and crying. I think in another moment I should have fallen."

"But you did not, Bessie. Are you glad?"

"I will tell you some time, not now."

He knew now how beautiful a gem he had found. Not a flaw made by false art. It had weaknesses, as all life must have, but they were natural and not cultivated. Holding her lightly and reverently, scarcely daring yet to kiss her unkissed lips, he vowed that no evil should come to her from him in word, or deed, or desire.

To her, the world had more good than evil, because she had more. The movement of the race was. upward. She knew there were evil shadows, but she seldom saw them. If she had she would have shone upon them with her purifying light. She believed in men. Consequently she believed in God. Necessarily, therefore, she believed in herself, and yet with humility.

But to our story. With a parting look over the deep Indian grave's edge, they turned toward the valley once more. They came soon upon the "hermit guide," sitting lonely upon a rock waiting, for them, but without comment, or even good-natured raillery.

He led them silently down and into the rustic pavilion. They urged him to play and sing.

"Oh, I'm no musician," he modestly protested.

"Ah, but we were here awhile ago, you must remember. We know."

He smiled thankfully for the compliment.

"I don't know anythin' to fit the occasion."

"Oh, the occasion is all right," said Merlin; "give us something lively."

"Would you object to a love song?" This very slyly.

"Not at all, if it ends well."

"I can't dew much without my old fiddle. I declare I must git the rest of them strings. A fiddle with only one string is a good deal like a

meule with a sore fut. It hain't much company.
But I'll try."

Their happy faces rejuvenated him. Quicker
and quicker flew his bow on the one string, firmer
grew the light of his flashing, steel eyes. With
a nervous little peck at his eyebrows, in the
middle of each verse, he gave himself up to such
comic songs as were most expressive of his sympathy and well wishes.

The first was the " Rose of Caroline." The first
verse ran something like this :

> I am happy as the morning, I am happy as the eve,
> I am a happy nigger all day long, I never sigh nor grieve,
> For I love a darling creature, whose form so light and fine,
> She's a gay gazelle, a beauty, is my Rose of Caroline.
> Features fair and curly hair, this charmer sealed my fate.
> I won my Rose of Caroline while swinging on the gate.

The *abandon* with which he threw himself into
the chorus was highly entertaining. With a swing
of the head and a steady tap of his foot he gave to
his song what so few people give to anything,
zest.

" I sing another. Mebbe you wouldn't like to
hear it."

" If it is as good as Rosy produce it." Merlin
was evidently in a better humor toward the
" hermit guide." Perhaps he felt that as a carpet
knight he would have suffered defeat; but that
the accompaniment of " falls," and ledge, and

5

rocks, and flower-colored nooks, had been of no small assistance to him. Anyway he was beaming. He caught himself keeping time all over to this queer song:

I'm over head and heels in love, the truth I'll tell, with a turtle-
    dove,
She ought to be in the skies above, an angel she should be.
Her laughing eyes with a dimpled chin, her face so sweet and
    fair,
She looks so neat and so complete with a mass of silk-like hair.
She's pretty as she dances on her pretty little toes,
She looks as neat and sweet as a little tuba rose.
She charms all the people as up the street she goes.
    She's my little sugar-plum.

"Well, that's my best. But then I don't charge you anything for it."

"I think we ought at least to take up a collection," suggested Bessie.

"No, indeed, never. You may not have noticed it sir," turning to Merlin, "but I am a Mason. Yes, sir, a free and accepted Mason. I've long had my eyes upon that Maltese cross on your chain, sir. *In. huc signit winches.* That's Latin, sir; genuine Latin. I may live out here in the meountins, but I know Latin when I see it. And I always fraternize with the brethren. Great thing that third degree. Hiram Abiff, the widder's son, was jest my sort. Any favors I can show you, sir, pleased to serve you. Always on the square."

Thus, out in the hills and wilds this odd man had learned the lesson of fraternity. He needed it.

Soon their carriage was bouncing along the rocky road toward Elizabethtown, eight miles away, where Merlin and Bessie were sojourning a few days before advancing to Keene valley, and on to Lake Placid by stage. The little brook running at their side, the twinkling stars just showing like bits of silver gray, the call of the valley farmer to his lazy herd on the slopes, and the memory-waking whip-poor-will far up on the ledges guarding his nest, all blended into a repose that came upon their happy lives like the soft look of a mother down upon the half-face of her babe, as she sings it to its sleep at her breast.

.   .   .   .

"But what will you do with your innocent little girl and her intense lover? Is not she too delicate for his world and his life?" We shall see.

Jack Tremain was as good natured a fellow as ever lived. He was a friend to everybody. Vagabonds, truly helpless unfortunates, and adventurers alike, had found him an easy prey. By reason of his social influence and wealth he had been a club-man of high degree at the University. A more selfish man might have come through, not much the worse for the wear, as the world estimates it; but Jack had been too easy in his friendships, and too generous in his judgments of men and women. I will not give the details of an unfortunate affair in which he became involved, and for which he had been "rusticated" in his junior year. Suffice it to say that among the little group of men and women of the town, into whose company Jack's club life had led him, was a woman several years his senior, but superbly handsome, and ruinously fascinating, when she set her head to win a coveted point. For more than a year Jack Tremain had been the point. She did not love him, she could not. It was not in her nature. But he was a great catch, was rich, and—well, she liked to know that men were talking about her and her daring breaks.

She soon found that Jack's ideals of womanhood were high in theory, however low some of them might be in practice. As much as was in her power she assumed a sort of dignified superiority to her surroundings when with him. She admitted to him the evil about her, but pretended to be carelessly indifferent to it. Her idea of morality could go no higher than that. So long as she was even negatively good she did not repel him.

He fell into some misunderstanding about this time with a club man which threatened to become very annoying to him. Matrice Bonner, by her strategic shrewdness, was able to settle the difficulty amicably—much against her personal pleasure, for "a quarrel in real life," as she called it, was a great delight to her. But she knew whence her gain in the matter would issue.

Jack overwhelmed her with gratitude. He forgot everything else about her except that she had greatly befriended him. He was her sworn friend from that day.

Little by little she undermined his manhood, his ideals, and his fate. Wine parties had no little to do with the final results. Never vicious, he had become at last simply weak, vacillating, yielding, moody, revengeful and gay by turns, as the occasion changed. At twenty-three he was simply a wreck on the shore of "high-life." Why "high" I do not know, unless it is because the fall is usually so marked and so fatal.

A month at home with his mother and sister had been his first strength for more than a year. He had gained one point; he was thoroughly convinced that he had been "worked." Nothing galls a man so much as the discovery of that fact—particularly if everyone else has discovered it too, and earlier. He had partially gained another point: that he had been guilty of great wrongs, both to his family and to himself. He knew the things done were evil; he was not quite sure that he had been wholly to blame.

This summer's outing had been planned for him and by him in part. He knew what it meant. His old-time love for his sister Bessie, returning now, had refreshed his ideals of womanhood. He had "looked on this picture and then on this," until he knew the difference between love and appetite.

He had assumed, perhaps from his knowledge of the world, a sort of watch-dog protection over her. He was her constant companion. It was thought that if he felt thus that her safety and pleasure depended solely upon him, as it would upon a journey like this, it would nerve him to resistance and duty, more than would an idle life at home. He had not drank since he returned. He had taken up his guitar again, and the old life seemed slowly creeping back.

Thus far on the route there had been nothing but pleasure. They had met a number of old friends, and had formed some new acquaintances, among whom was Merlin Hall. He and Jack found good fellowship at once. In fact, Jack gave Bessie over to him almost from the first. This may have been the cause of his fall.

Merlin and Bessie reached the Windsor House in time for a late supper, though they were both too much excited for hunger.

"I must see Jack right away. I suppose in the absence of other authorities I must look to him for confirmation of my rash act," said Merlin.

"I'm so glad for Jack's sake."

"And not for your own, Bessie?"

"You know what I mean."

"Yes, I do; and we will lift the poor boy out.

I had a long talk with him only yesterday. He told me his only fear now was of that woman. He said he trembled at every corner lest he should meet her. He made me promise that I would take him away and hide him if she should find us. He thinks she is hunting him up."

"God pity him if she is! What a life! What becomes of a woman's soul do you think when she falls to such a level!"

"She damns it."

"Beyond hope, do you think?"

"If deeds are to be the judgment test."

"But may there not be mercy? Is not one's heredity and early training taken into the evidence? Surely it must."

"Probably, when one's fall is through the machinations of others, and because of some inherited weakness. But for premeditated, calculating debauchery of body and soul, deeds must decide. Such a man fixes his life in evil, and loves it. He ought to possess it forever."

"But do they never have any remorse? Do they feel no longings for release? Suppose you should read 'Beyond the Gates,' to such a woman as Matrice Bonner, would it have no effect?"

"Yes, she would laugh at you, and call you an 'innocent little chit,' but missing life's real meaning."

"Do you think she would dare?"

"I think she would."

"If you could tell her the story of Romola —"

"The probabilities are that if the Savior Himself were here, and were to give her choice between your life and seven devils, she would take the devils."

"I don't believe any soul on earth is so depraved."

"I am glad you don't. That's one reason I love you."

"Because you think I am so ignorant?"

"No, but because you are so pure yourself. By the way, do you remember that sweet couplet of Emerson's Threnody:

'Hearts are dust, hearts' loves remain,
Heart's love will meet thee again.'

It has been in my ears with the roar of the falls ever since I found you sobbing on the rocks. Oh, Bessie, just to think —"

"Let's don't think—about that. Go on with Emerson."

"Do you know, I believe in Emerson as a poet; he did not concern himself much about rhythm, but his creative imagination is matchless. There has been but one other in all our literature, and she did so little verse, that one scarcely ever thinks of her as a poet. Dear Helen Hunt. I have always liked that better than her wedded name. I have a strong autograph-letter showing her at her best, which I will send you after I return home, also a pair of scraps from Emerson's pen. To me they are priceless."

"Speaking of Emerson calls to my mind a new volume of Carlyle which I read recently. It is an assortment of notes made by some one on a series of lectures on literature delivered several years before his death. I found it very unsatisfactory. One might as well try to take the Niagara by dictation, as to transmit Carlyle by notes."

"The new Isaiah. He was to England what Tolstoi is to Russia. A different type of man, as one would naturally expect. Russian institutions and philosophy could never make a Carlyle."

"Nor English a Tolstoi."

"Oh, he might do after Wannamaker had trimmed him up a little."

"He wears glasses. I am told they are blue."

"Wannamaker, you mean?"

"Certainly."

"The Russian sees things as they are in Russia. He knows but little of the domestic life in a civilized land like ours. His censors should read his 'Work While it is Yet Day,' if they still doubt his ideals of home life."

"Are all the masters aged or dead, in America?"

"A hundred disciples have arisen for every master. That is better; it is more democratic. Then too, just now, the theme of a book has become more significant than the author's name. Take it in sociology for instance, and we care more that we have Social Phases of Christianity, Murvale Eastman, Jason Edwards, A Hazard of New Fortunes, and How the Other Half Lives, than that we have an Ely, Tourgee, Garland, Howells or Riis. The book is vital now. Does it help on the evolution of things? If not, it has no *raison d'etre.* But Jack must be in by this time. He usually comes to the parlor. He may have gone up to his room. I will slip up and see. If I am not back in ten minutes don't wait. Good night, my love." A soft little pressure of her clinging hand was all.

Five minutes had not passed, when he returned with a peculiar but resolute look on his face. Slipping quite to her side and stooping, he said softly, but calmly: "Come up to Jack's room, Bessie. He needs us both."

She knew as well as though he had told her all. Jack had slipped. But perhaps they could catch him before he lost every hold.

"Is she here?" she whispered as she clung to his arm on the stairs.

"She has been here, but I hope she is gone."

"I want to see her now, that she is here."

"You see her, Bessie?"

"Yes, I must."

"Well, you know best."

Poor Jack lay upon the couch moaning. He had not drank enough to bring on stupor, but just enough, now that the first gay mood was gone, to leave him wretched and undone.

"Oh, Bessie, why didn't you stay here? I thought I was all right. I ran up here the moment I saw her, but she followed me. I was weak enough to let her in. It was all over then. Keep her out. There has something gone wrong. She looks terrible. I should never have known her but for her eyes. She is desperate about something."

"Keep quiet, Jack," said Bessie, soothingly, taking his fine head upon her knees and kissing him. "I won't leave you any more, and Jack, Merlin has come to stay, too. He wants you to congratulate him, though I don't see why he should expect any one to do that." So perfect was her love that it seemed not at all immodest to talk of it.

Jack looked up with a feeble smile.

"This time yesterday how pleased I would have been to hear it. But to-day—my God, how did I let it happen!"

"Keep up, old fellow," said Merlin, sitting on the edge of the couch. "No one knows it but Bessie and me. We'll prop you. You'll be able to go alone by-and-by."

"She knows it, and that's the devil of it—excuse me, but that's just the situation!"

"I'm going to see her myself, Jack."

"Good God! you, Bessie? Never. I'll murder her if she speaks to you."

He was thoroughly excited now. It was good for him. This revulsion of feeling would not pass away without some permanent results.

"You must let me have my way in this, Jack."

"What does she mean, Merlin?"

"I give it up, Jack, and you had better. She will have her way in spite of us," with a reassuring twinkle in his eyes.

"She said she would be back at nine. I don't know why she went away. There's something up."

"It is nine now," said Bessie. "You take Jack to your room; I will remain here until she comes."

"Bessie you must not do it. Think what she is."

"I have thought of all. I shall stay."

A knock. An open door. Two women face to face. One much surprised, the other very calm.

"Come in; my brother Jack will be back soon. He was not feeling well, and is resting with a friend."

Matrice Bonner had never yielded before. She did now. She sat upon the couch where she had left Jack an hour before.

"Are you his sister?" she ventured.

"Yes, Jack's my only brother. My first recollection is of his holding me while we sat in the old swing. There was a little place between his soft neck and his firm shoulder, where my head could just lie, while he held it from bobbing with his warm chin."

Impulsive natures act rapidly. Something in that baby picture touched the proud woman. Or, there may have been weeks of preparation for this one final influence. She threw up her hands with a look of intense pain, and as they fell, clasping them tight, let her head sink lower and lower, until Bessie imagined she had swooned. Going to her very quietly, she placed both her hands on her temples to lift her head. As though stung by the touch, she lifted her face and leaned back with flashing eyes. Then with a pitiful, hunted look in them, cried :

"Do you touch me ? And do you know who I am ?"

"You are a woman. You are in distress. I have forgotten the rest."

"Oh, why should help always come too late ?"

"I wonder if it is ever too late."

"What do you mean ?"

"Tell me all your trouble. It is nothing light, I am sure."

"Light, if the rocks and mountains of the judgment day shall be light."

"Tell me of the past and present. When we get them straight, the future is already straight."

She hesitated, looked with mesmeric, searching

eyes into Bessie's trustful face, as though determined to find what subtle motive lay back of her winning ways. The look satisfied her. She told all.

She had secretly married one of the club men soon after Jack was sent home, with the agreement that at the end of a year, when he should become of age, and heir to great estates, he was to acknowledge her as his wife. The year had passed. He had deserted her. Something was wrong with the marriage certificate. It would cost hundreds of dollars to attempt to establish her claim. Her babe was two months old. She was penniless, and "out of the swim." Grown desperate over the hunger of her babe, half frenzied herself, friendless, too proud to beg, and with no room to work with her infant, as a last resort she had come after Jack, having seen by accident the notice of his proposed visit to the mountains, and the route. She had pawned her last piece of jewelry, a bracelet Jack had given her, that she might make the journey. Her purpose had simply been to appeal to him for help, until she could get strong enough to fight her way bitterly through. But as she talked to him, the old spirit came back, a yearning to forget the awful present. She had but to suggest it in a moment's weakness, and the wine was ordered. As she drank, instead of gaiety, remorse came. Jack soon became tender, as was his wont when under the influence of liquor. She could not bear his embraces, and abruptly left him, promising to return when he had sobered up a little, and then make known her real mission.

"I have told you all. I never dreamed I should have told it just as it was to Jack, much less to a woman, and that woman his sister. I have been a proud, stubborn woman. I am broken now. Here on my knees I beg mercy for my baby's sake. I have held his poor little head under my chin, just as Jack used to hold yours, his little hot hands twitching in mine. My heart is breaking now as I think of him left alone with the coarse and filthy nurse who is keeping him for me. She may be drunk this very minute, and my boy dead; my poor white-faced little lamb! God pity him, and pity me. You must know I had a woman's respect after all for your brother, that I should venture to him with this awful message. Think of a proud woman hunting her old lover to beg a crust for herself and babe, the ruins of another man's passion. Your eyes are soft as an angel's. Surely they will pity me. What can I do? where shall I go? Anything and anywhere, in the wide world, only so that I can keep my baby and give him bread. Tell me. Don't forsake me. I will do anything you say."

What a life was this drifting wreck! A dismantled hulk floating so near a white-sailed vessel. Would it plunge the trim little ship down with its woeful weight, or would there be sail enough to put both into harbor?

Had Bessie been anything less than a pure-souled, earnest woman, she would have been tempted to scorn this appeal, or turn away in dismay. Being both, she said nothing about "depravity," "the wages of sin," "the way of the transgressor," "the Magdalene's Home" or "the Orphans' Asylum."

Must I write it? Will the reader finish my story? He shall read this next sentence, and it shall not fade from his memory forever.

"Poor, broken-winged bird, your flying was too bold, the rocks were hard. You are a woman, and the mother of a hungry babe. I love you, and I will not leave nor forsake you."

Farewell, Priest; farewell, Levite. The Good Samaritans will keep me close company to the end.

When Jack and Merlin had heard the story, as Bessie alone could tell it, they sat so still they heard the little silver clock on the table tick a hundred times or more.

Merlin never felt so sharply before the reality of Time. It was a trying moment to Bessie as to each of the others. She had repeated to them her resolution and promise. What would Merlin say? Would it end their just-begun relationship? It

would test him, that much she knew. If he did
not bear it, then she had mistaken him. To know
it now were far better than to discover it little by
little, and too late.

She waited. Her heart got the same measure
the clock had. Would they never speak? It came
at last, like a far-away voice out of the shadows
of the unlighted room, half choking, as though
shamedly struggling to show no womanly weakness: "Bessie,—you—are—the noblest—woman—
this side—of heaven." It was Merlin's voice.
"Amen!" added Jack. It was the most religious
thing he had done since he left home three years
before.

Bessie felt she must cry. The strain had been
too hard. Had the answer been different, she
would not have shed a tear. How joyous it was to
feel them gushing through her fingers as she
pressed her face. But when her lover, never so
dear to her as now, took them away in his own
strong hands, and kissed both her cheeks, tears
and all, and holding her to him sealed for the first
time his vows of the day, it was heaven let down
beneath stars.

But that poor, waiting, troubled heart without!
She must go to her. Kissing Jack, she whispered
to him the "open sesame" of his permanent recovery: "Devote the coming year to this poor
woman and her baby, Jack. See that she gets up
again. Give her courage, and keep yourself un-

6

spotted from the world." The heroic in his soul came out in bold relief, in quick response.

Matrice makes her own living and her boy Jack's. She sings at her work. No great ambition stirs her. To have a home and watch her baby boy, and keep his face bright and his heart clean, is her highest ambition. To-day has been a particularly happy one for the mother and the boy. His "Aunt Bessie," and both his uncles, Jack and Merlin, and little cousin, baby Matrice, have been with them all day. The delicate repast, all the work of Matrice's hands, at the close of the afternoon, was but one more proof of the calmness and the cleanness of her life without and within.

No evil has come into Bessie's simple life. More than one demon of lust and hate has fled at her approach.

So does the Miracle Worker of Galilee "do greater works than these," through his own.

"Ye are my friends." Oh, sweet Galilean! to be Thy friend is to be friendly to the whole World.

A WOMAN?

CHAPTER I

ACROSS Mirror Lake the angle of the " Baldwin" lights squared the irregular water line. To the left a tower of light rose above the "Stephen's." Directly to the right round Cobble rose into the night, as the head of a wondering child at play rises above the grass, to " spy the coast." Back behind all, one cheek alone partly visible in the moon-smitten night, lay White Face, most striking and popular of the Adirondacks. In the nearer distance, but hidden, Lake Placid slept beside the wind-singing pines, while one kept thinking of the white, dead spruces just in its water's edge, standing like ghostly sentinels.

" I know I am wrong, and that it is more like a bear than a man to say it, but I wish you wouldn't, Elaine."

" Don't you like music ?"

" Yes."

" And—and—me ?"

" How can you ask ?"

" Well, don't we blend, music and I, and your—love ?"

"Certainly, my dear ; but don't you see the difference ? Music and yourself in my own home—I can pray for nothing more ; but your music and you in a public drawing-room, or—or—, upon the concert stage, is what distresses me, and a crowd of men staring at you, and not speechless either, I can assure you."

"Why, Maxwell Harley! would you have them blind and dumb ?"

It was in a shadowy corner of the broad veranda of the Mirror Lake Hotel, just up the spreading slope from Mirror Lake. The speakers had evidently been upon good terms, to say the least. Elaine Humeston was a rising young cornetist of Boston. Max Harley was her admirer, and it would seem from what we have just heard, an accepted lover. Of his love for her there could be no doubt. As between her love and her music there were occasionally vexing doubts, particularly when, as now, he sought to divide her life. She had accepted an invitation from the proprietor of the hotel, an old friend, for the season of—well, a nameless season. She had done so because she needed the hills and the pure air. Her half invalid mother needed them more. They were not rich. Her career had just begun. As usual, the expenses of the few brief tours she had made with two of her Boston musical friends, under the management of the brother of one of them, had kept pretty even pace with the revenue. She seized

as a gift from heaven this opportunity for rest and
pleasure with her pale, but sweet-faced mother.
That she herself must often play for the hotel
guests, sometimes even for their dancing, had not
troubled her in the least, except, when talking it
over with Harley one evening, instead of the congratulations she expected, there came a puzzling
frown, and a commonplace remark which could
have no bearing whatever upon the, to her, all-
absorbing matter. A summer in the Adirondacks
and at Lake Placid, and Max not enthusiastic!

Of course she had expected a lover's protest
against so long an absence, some half-pouting en-
dearment; but his chilling silence was more than
a prohibition. Then she remembered his old heart
ailment: "She was his, and not the property of
the public." She did not congeal easily. Indeed
she could be very warming when the air grew too
chill for her comfort. Max left in a better humor.
In that sort of a humor a man works himself into—
works is the word I want to use—when he knows
the woman he loves has come to a decision; and
if he would not be omitted entirely from its issues,
he must, with more or less grace, yield.

Man is a queer animal. Even if he is to suffer
defeat, he likes to be on the field when the fight
is on. Just two weeks after Elaine had settled
herself and the dear little mother in a cosy corner
of their summer home, with a soothing view of the
quiet lake and quieter hills, imagine her surprise,

half glad, half painful, to find herself face to face
with Max Harley as she walked one evening to
the grand Chickering in the great parlor, her fingers closely clasped about her silver pet.

"Maxwell Harley!"

She always added the "well" when surprised,
or attempting unusual dignity.

"O yes, it's I. Thought I would run up for a
couple of days. Town is confounded still.
Nothing in motion but the river, and an occasional
train. Took one, and here I am. Fine place."

"Have you just come?"

"Yes. Came by stage from Saranac."

"Beautiful drive, isn't it?"

"Didn't see it."

"Didn't see it?"

"No—I—I was in somewhat of a hurry."

"Oh! Well, come into the parlor, Max, I must
play for an hour, and then we—I will be free.
There is a mammoth whist party on for the evening, and they won't need much music to-night."

She turned without giving him time to protest.
She was a woman, a budding professional woman,
and had learned already to keep her business engagements, a rare quality which I have noticed in
every professional woman of my acquaintance. It
is a sort of unreasoning fidelity to her word. Perhaps I am wrong in the adjective—a conscience
fidelity, I should call it.

For an hour Max sat in a distant corner. The

only sympathy he showed with the beautiful cornetist was unconscious; he kept his huge chair
rocking in perfect time with her music. He sat
apart, as though ashamed of her. She was conscious of it all. She never played with such zest.
The guests gathering about the card tables, and
receiving their delicately-ribboned ivory souve-
nirs, paused to listen. Already the favorite of
every one, she seemed to hold them with a firmer
grasp just now.

She was worthy of their wondering admiration
in every way. Not alone in her music was she
graceful and expressive. Tall, with the grace and
symmetry of the hemlock, pliant, thrilling with
health, she walked like a queen along the polished floors of the great drawing-rooms. Not as
a dominant queen, but queenly by her unconscious
power. Her sweet-faced modesty was made strong
with a soldierly bearing her father gave her before
he fell at Chickamauga in '63. Every child in
the company loved her; not as children love for
bon bons, but as they cling for a kiss.

Never was she so full of power and grace as
to-night. She was playing the familiar "prison
song" from Il Trovatore, so old, and yet always
calling the heart from every other emotion. It
was the background to-night for her joy; a foil
to her happiness. To be sure, Max was not *en-
rapport*. But love conquers so easily.

Standing, her white satin slipper firmly set upon

the soft velvet rug, she swayed with the rhythm of her music until the electric lights hung like great glistening mists before the tearful eyes of her thrilled audience. Even Max felt himself giving way under the spell. But the burst of applause as she sat down brought back the old jealousy. He rose in rather an ungallant manner to meet her, as she drew near him, he and she now the center of all attention.

"Shall we go out now, and see if we can find a star?" she asked tremulously, for the passion of her music had not subsided. She so hoped it might blend into the other and become a part of it to-night—if only he wouldn't look so glum.

"These people seem to think they have found one here," he replied. He was trying to be complimentary; the words were; the tone, anything else.

She took his arm and they escaped out to the sweeping piazza, through a group of admirers waiting to repeat their kind words of other evenings. There the reproachful words at the beginning of the story were spoken.

"If a woman has a gift, and you insist that I have, why should she put it in a napkin? or, to be more realistic, in a dish-rag? or why should appreciation of it by others be any more a disgrace than when a man has the power to please or help?"

"Simply because a woman is something more

than any gift. Something else, by her very nature,
is the prominent element of her life. With men
their gifts are their best, sometimes their all. We
are willing to let a man live as he chooses, if only
he will paint us good pictures or write us real
verses. But a woman must be—well, womanly, vir-
tuous above all."

"Virtue is distinctly a womanly quality, then? I
had not expected you would admit as much."

"You know what I mean; virtue and genius are
not synonymous. A woman must have the first.
A man may have either, but must have the latter,
if he succeed."

"He rarely has both, then, you think?"

"Oh, you take me too literally."

"I simply took your words. You know mind-
reading is not my gift."

"Come, Elaine, we must not do this. I came
here for my loneliness. The moonlight is too soft
for harsh words." Taking her hand and catching
the thrill of her aroused spirit, he longed to take
her into his arms and hush all questionings. But
she seemed to feel that a crisis was upon them.
Her mind was quickened into bolder thought than
usual, and she went on.

"You must surely admit that a woman's virtue
need not be spoiled by the possession of inferior
gifts; particularly the gifts of the fine arts."

"Not the possession of them, surely, but such use

of them as will bring her into the polluted currents of the world's life."

It was with a tinge of scorn, and you will forgive her, that she replied, directing his attention through the open windows to the scene within.

"Those innocent girls at the card-tables are not in the polluted current, are they? Last night they danced, some of them, with more than a score of men, the most of whom they never saw before. Were they in the current, or out of it? You know I am not opposed to their doing it. I do it myself. But I simply was curious to know whether you thought them safe and only myself unsafe."

"Oh, Elaine, you are so persistent. Of course you are safe here. This is a choice company of men and women. I presume none of them are vampires. But this is only the beginning of a public life which will soon carry you out into the full currents of the common people, where you know there is every species of contaminating ill."

"As I understand your philosophy, then, it is that a man or woman will surely fall away from virtue if once in the active world. Man *may* do so, but if he possess genius may still succeed. Woman can not."

"Something like that, only I don't mean that every woman would become depraved, but that the public would so regard her, simply because she was out of her place. And I must confess, too, that I believe any woman under such influences would fall into hard, worldly ways of thinking, would grow more and more a stranger to womanly affection and purposes, and become more masculine and unattractive."

"Public opinion is still your criterion, is it? And delicate, fancy-work, hysterical women are still your ideals! I so scorn the one, when I face duty, and so detest the others, that I fear lest we be unable to find mutually congenial friendships."

"Elaine, you must not say that. You know you are my ideal woman. I dislike weak, and admire strong women, just as much as you do."

"Strong in what? Mere negative virtue? By the way, what is this virtue you worship before? Is it something in nature apart from one's faculties and accomplishments? A resident inheritance in a small portion of the human family? I have thought virtue was character, and character is as varied as men are. Yours is the sum of your capabilities and their uses. Mine is no less. If yours is to plead for justice for men, to be criticised, probably hated by the lawless and oppressive, why not mine, in keeping myself unspotted from the world, to make it forget its sullen selfishness, and sing to itself of noble living under my leading? Or is it the prerogative of man alone to lead and help the many? woman's to lead and help the two or three of her household, and that with sixteenth century limitations?"

"But you would unsex the race, my dear."

"Perhaps it needs a little unsexing. If woman's sphere is fixed by her sex to be either domestic service or the gratifying of the smaller and more ignoble propensities of men ; if she can only suffer and then see another accomplish ; if her work and glory, yes, and immortality, are forever to be by proxy, because of her sex; if man must always be master and director, and the winner of all good things by reason of his sex, then to unsex the race were not a bad mission. If I remember correctly, the ideal relations of men and women, as announced by the Great Teacher, are to know no distinction of sex ; while the life beyond is declared to be wholly without sex relations, even marriage itself being abrogated. If these be ideal, then to make the whole lives of men and women gravitate about two wholly dissimilar centers, with a dead line between, is to disprove evolution. And ideals are never to be attained.

"But it is false. All life is one, differing in minor details, but common in essentials. The same elements are in manhood and womanhood."

"I confess that seems as true as strange to me."

"Then neither man nor woman can succeed without virtue. Genius in either case can only enhance virtue. If the virtue depart, it is not on account of genius, but in spite of it."

"Well, I didn't come all this way, Elaine, to become a convert to woman's rights. There is one woman right, just right, and she is right here. Let us see the lake wooing the moon. Perhaps it will change our mood."

"If I have seemed earnest, Max, it is because I have no higher ambition in the world than to have my life measure with yours. I will not be a dwarf. If I may not be of your stature, I will not walk beside you."

"Elaine, I have no impulse, no thought, no will, that does not already and always look up to find your face and its approval. Here by the still water of this centuried lake, constant through the infinite variety of its moods, contented and restful in the enlocking arms of these trusty hills, at peace with the world, I again and again give all, reserving no thought, no emotion, all, to thee, Elaine. I would not limit a gift of yours any more than I would strangle a babe at its mother's breast. I do not always see with your eyes, nor think with your brain. You would not have me do so. But, and perhaps I have learned it fully just to-night, I do not want you to see with my eyes, nor think with my brain. My devoutest wish is that we may see the same things. So endeth the first lesson—severe in the lettering, sweet and helpful in the sentence. If to-morrow you will teach me another, as simple and as trusting, I will be your most grateful pupil."

"And you will never doubt me again, Max; I mean my ambitions, my real motive in life?"

"Not again."

"Then I am doubly glad you came."

For a long time they sat, lulled into absolute peace by the communing waves, laughingly shying back and forth at their feet, clapping their tiny hands, wringing their fairy-like fingers in mock astonishment, lisping crooning little baby words, and dancing time to the gentle wind's ballads. Out and beyond, the dimly waving line of the hills rose higher and higher into the heavens, a shadowy way for the soul's ascent. Lake, river and sea; plain, hills, and mountain; earth and sky and stars, each a new expression of the Infinite, were, after all, one vast universe. Aye, universe and Infinite were not parts, but One. So, too, their different and changing hopes, and faiths, and endeavors were one communion, one love, and one life. Was not the Infinite in them both? Did they not both worship Him in His hills, and stars, and reason?

CHAPTER II.

THE Lakes were aquiver with the new day, the hill-sides were gardens of the birds, as Max and Elaine started out for Lake Placid, a sharp little walk from the hotel.

"Now for the second lesson," said Harley.

"Don't let's 'scuss anything to-day, Max."

"We won't; we'll just talk, and if I learn any-thing I hope I'll have the grace to say so."

They stopped a moment to look back upon the sweeping horizon so far away.

"Can you see The Pass yonder between McIntyre and Wall Face? It seems impossible that we are so close to that remote savagery of the red men. Every hill has been tracked with their trails."

"And their women have raised corn in these very valleys. That's woman's rights for you, Elaine."

"How can you be so cruel?"

"I didn't mean it."

"Anyway, the argument is mine. Their women were slaves, too, their lords simply gave them different tasks from some of ours. I don't know; I believe I would prefer raising corn to domestic service. Not that I dislike housework or home life. I love it. Mamma and I always do our own work when I am at home. But to know nothing else, and to be compelled to do it as the only way of pleasing your master—that, never!"

"Well, you needn't."

"Here is the public library. Let us take some books with us; you may want to read to me."

"What shall we select?"

"Oh, something appropriate. Here is Sanborn's 'John Brown.' By the way, we must visit John Brown's grave before we return. It lies a few miles back, on the road to Keene Valley. I have an irresistible longing to sing 'John Brown's body lies a-mouldering in the grave," over his very dust."

" You might see his soul go marching on."

" I feel it now. Liberty is in the air, even for us poor slaves of the hearth."

" Don't. I can hear your chains clanking now."

" No, that's just the trouble. You men don't hear them. It's like the hum of insects or the ticking of a clock, you've gotten used to it."

" Ah! here is Bishop Potter's ' Way-Marks.' You honor the dead, and I will remember the living."

" Do you know, Lake Placid would not be what it is without the Potters? A true friend to liberty, the Bishop is, too."

" I am sorry now I took it. With you on the one hand, and John Brown and the Bishop on the other, I fear an ambush. But I love Sanborn's musical lines so well I can lose myself in them and escape. I was under the spell of his poetic fervor for two summers at Concord, when Alcott was still living and called together his Transcendental Saints in the Orchard School of Philosophy. Next to the old Vegetarian, I admired Sanborn. Gentle, tender, far-seeing, but close to one all the while, leading you by easy stages a long way out toward the soul of things. It was like the starting up of a cool breeze after Plato and Hegel's disciples had exhausted the oxygen, to have Sanborn talk. He knew the poets as brothers. He and Herbert were kindred souls."

" There you can see Placid through the pines. I wonder they don't take those dead stumps away. This approach is distressingly marred by them. We must go farther up. Here is the trail to an old camp. It leads to a quiet spot."

" Lead on, thou rejuvenated Indian maiden, returned to teach these nineteenth century bucks the emancipation of woman !"

" Hush ! you will frighten the birds."

A mocking little thrush peeped, and laughed to himself. He too had loved. That wouldn't frighten him; oh, no. These were lovers' woods. To be sure, he did the singing, and provided the worms, but a submissive little lord was he. He was neither master nor slave. Not even nature belies her impulse of freedom. What nature speaks in instinct, revelation never denies in law. Man alone perverts both instinct and law.

" Here, I think, you see Placid at its best. Northeast is Moose Island, and West Lake is just beyond. I sat here one evening last week while a cloud hung over White Face, against which the setting sun made, not a rainbow, but a square of tints. It was evidently an end of what would have been a huge bow had there been cloud enough. But every tint was there. I thought of it as life in outline. Every soul, no matter how

7

limited or cut off by its environment, has in it the primary colors. Other lives, however lengthened and arched by education and culture, cannot by any means add an eighth color."

"A pretty picture, my dear."

"Truer even than pretty. It is not a question as to whether men or women shall do this or that. It is, whether any person shall be permitted to do anything which any other is not permitted to do. Shall not law, and custom, and creed come to be the same for all men at last? Is it any worse for the few to rule, than for the few to make the laws, or to establish doctrine?"

"But are the people capable?"

"No. But children fed upon soup sicken at meat. If you had always been told that you were idiotic, or untrustworthy, or born with a certain bent of character, you would have believed it after a while, and lived it too. It is as though I were to cage that mountain thrush yonder and say to it every morning: 'Fly, you idler. Don't you know what wings are for? Don't droop your head. Shame upon you! See what gifts God has bestowed upon you! You need only to use them. See where others of your kind have flown and builded their nests. Fly!'"

"But many of the 'caged birds' do fly. Witness the children of poverty who have become rich or great."

"Yes, the cage has not been as strong as some

would have it. Now and then an over-zealous
prisoner has broken out and has risen in spite of
his imprisonment."

I wish you could have seen the fine scorn on this
young girl's face. We have studied her at the re-
spectful distance of the hotel parlor, let us look at
her now with her lover's eyes. Notice first her
peculiar mouth ; as sweet as a baby's at the corners, but firm as a soldier's two thirds of its
breadth. Max always wanted to kiss her where
the curves turned into dimples on either side of
her beautiful chin. Her hazel eyes are far apart
but large, covered with full lids and long, sweeping lashes. They make her face like tinted marble when she sleeps, like irresistible, half divine
energy when she wakes. In the cornea there is
the tint of the bluebells, giving them that delicacy
of expression unpicturable. Her forehead, too
noble for the current idea of beauty, is partially
hidden by a roll of glossy hair hanging carelessly
free—not a bang, how gratefully do I record it !
To see this head with its queenly poise, was to
know that it was incapable of any small thoughts.
Her superb figure bears out the indication of her
face and head. Even the very tips of her fingers
are expressive of fine feeling, fine execution. A
nobility which will protect her like a circle of fire
anywhere in America clothes her like a garment.
Max is convinced of this at last ; still a homesick-

ness hurts him all over when he thinks of her as the servant of the people.

"Elaine, I cannot, cannot give you to the world. You are mine, eyes, voice, soul, every gift."

"Maxwell, I cannot, cannot give you to the world. You are mine, eyes, voice—"

"Don't."

"But you see where it ends. Men can praise, admire, and employ you, but not your wife."

"But the family must have sustenance and protection. Man alone can furnish that."

"Do you think so? It is not difficult to imagine your loss of health—a reality if you don't rest more, Max. It would be no disgrace then for me to earn money, would it?"

"Certainly not. Nor for yourself and mother now."

"Well, then is it not a matter of pride more than a matter of 'eternal fitness,' that you men insist upon earning all of the living? But after all, do we not do as much to earn it, when we do our part in domestic service? The only difference in this latter course is that we do our share of the labor, often more, but have no share in the emoluments or even in the development of the husband's life—except by proxy. The moon is very sweet, and subdued, shining by the reflected light of the sun—but, thanks, I prefer to be a star at least, and shine in my own light."

"But the home life, its duties and burdens, who shall bear them?"

"The wife and mother. First, she ought to be a willing wife, and no less a willing mother. Then her work for the world should be no more than her inclinations, her time, and her capacity will fit her for. Woman asks for nothing more than that she shall be permitted to do anything she can within the sex line limitation. Little by little she has worked her way into the arts, trades and professions; into the colleges and universities. She cannot stop here. An education, a created ambition, with nothing to gratify it, means animalism. She *must* go on. But there ought to be but one test for men and women alike: Can she, can he, do this work? Yes; then she, then he, ought."

"Very fine, my little reformer, I agree. That saves me. No one can go starring across the continent when her husband's garments are in tatters. I can imagine you lifting the people up to 'Home, Sweet Home,' after getting a telegram like this: 'Come home, bread sour, buttons off, the maid eloped.—M. H.'"

"I did not want to have to tell you, Max, that no ambition of mine shall ever tempt me to a thought of leaving my home uncared for. I shall be a fixed star. In music and art, and in every way, I shall seek to be helpful to my own city, already so kind to my poor gifts. But I shall ex-

pect from you no prolonged absences, professional
or otherwise. We shall be at home together, we
shall go abroad together. But I promise you now
I shall figure in every case you plead, and in the
acceptance of cases as well as in the pleading.
They say there is nearly always a woman in every
lawsuit. There shall be one in all yours. I have
been secretly reading law for more than a year.
How do you like it?"

"If I were to sue for a divorce, you would figure
double, wouldn't you?"

"Possibly treble, for I would certainly plead
my own case. But if I have health,. and your
help, I mean that the world shall never think of
Maxwell Harley without also thinking of his wife.
I mean it very modestly, Max, but I mean it most
thoroughly."

"I believe you, and believe in you. I would not
have it otherwise, if I could. But say, Elaine, you
won't vote, will you?"

"Yes, if we live in Boston. Not that I think
the ballot is the outer circle of woman's sphere;
it is only incidental to it. The great thing is
equality. Spiritual—that is conceded. Mental—
we assume it. Physical—God wills it; not in
strength, but in the rights of body."

"I have it now; the lecture field. We'll take
an evening together. Joint discussion, say. You
deny, and I'll affirm the proposition: 'Is man
woman's equal in any sense?'"

"You will need to read up zealously to prove it."

"Oh, just in sport, you know. I'll step out at the close, and admit that I am defeated, that I really take the same side that my wife does."

"You would need to do that to set the audience square with you mentally, Max."

"Why will you be so stinging?"

"Because I'm your honey bee, I guess."

"I wish you would attend to the honey part a little more carefully."

He leaned toward her with such yielding tenderness, she forgot all else but that she loved him. The little thrush suddenly bethought him of a leafly bower, where an unguarded nest held a very lonesome mother bird. With a faintly-twittered pang over his neglect, he flew to his own love-tree, the air vibrant with his vocal joy.

So endeth the second lesson.

Clouds filed into solemn line from White Face to Marcy, and beyond to Hurricane. Quietly as death comes in, unannounced, the battalions of heaven were wheeled into line for action. The lake was lead in motion and color. Every bird-voice was hushed. One could almost hear the beating of his heart. The Adirondacks were asleep.

But the enemy stole on apace. A gleam of swords, sunbright, but not the sound of a rattling wheel or rolling drum. Again and again the tempest swords gleamed like some mighty pre-battle drill. Now low over the distant hills the rumble of a nearer approach is heard. The whistling fife-winds suddenly herald the rapid on-coming. Before one can think, or turn, with dash and fury, with hissing rain like shot, and crashing boughs shaking like spears, with push and blinding smiting of sheeted water, the storm hordes are upon the earth. The lake rushes here and there for escape. The trees dodge in blind frenzy only to lean into the arms of the grasping tornado. Too frightened to cry out, the earth is dumb, in bug, and bird, and beast. It bows to the enemy and surrenders.

Between the mists and parting branches might have been seen, could one have faced the tempest, a man and a woman. They were standing with bowed heads in the midst of the battle of elements, quiet, waiting, filled, in spite of the danger, with awe before such superb grandeur. Neither was braver than the other, neither clung alone to the other. Each sheltered, each fortified the other.

The Universe is one whether in storm or calm. All is one. They were one.

CHAPTER III.

Poor John Hedderson is on trial for his life, charged by the State of Massachusetts with deliberately shooting one Stepen Miller, a Pinkerton detective, while, in company with a hundred of his

band, endeavoring to get possession of the Union
Woolen Mills.. Not only had the employes been
forced to a reduction in wages of twelve per cent.
under a plea of a falling market, but it was beyond
question another pooled effort on the part of capital to break into fragments the Amalgamated
Association of labor. The men had struck peace-
ably, but resolutely, saying they and their families were confronting starvation now; it were better
to die for their rights and for the future, than to
starve. They would do no damage to the property,
but none should work but their own.

In a bloodhound attempt to drive them away the
Pinkertons had been shipped into the grounds.
After a slight skirmish they were driven back;
several had been wounded, one Stephen Miller, was
killed. A policeman standing, no one knew where,
swore John Hedderson fired the fatal shot. He is
on trial, indicted by the Grand Jury for murder in
the first degree. Powerful legal talent is arrayed
against him. So common has become the feeling
against the Pinkertons, so bitterly are they hated
by the workingmen, that this is to be made a test
case. The slayer must be hung, or their days of
service are numbered.

Maxwell Harley is Hedderson's attorney. He is
alone. The poor fellow has no money and the treasury of the association is nearly empty on account of
the long strike. No, not alone. Every brief, every
decree of the higher courts, the impeachment of the

police officer, every extenuating circumstance in
the prisoner's position and relation to the affray,
have been scrutinized, corrected, and the advocate
himself filled with inspiration by a noble woman
bringing her intuition, her legal learning, and,
above all, her sympathies, her whole nature into
the case. That woman is Elaine Harley. Beside
her husband at the opening of the case, two-thirds
of his jury selections were made by her final decision. She seemed to read every man as he stood
for examination. Every hour of the trial she has
supplied notes and references ; in cross-examina-
tion twice her whispered questions have proved
fatal to the prosecution.

On the morning of her husband's address to the
jury she has filled him with an almost religious
devotion to his cause, and a resolute affection for
his client and his overpowered brethren. The vast
audience wondered what impassioned orator had
been suddenly let down among them. The mil-
lionaire proprietors of the mills fidgeted, sneered,
reddened, paled, trembled before his denunciation
of the power of monopoly, and the unjust purchas-
ing power of money. Men in coarse clothes wept
like children in a death-chamber, sobbing piteously
as though with bursting throats, while he pictured
their hardships, struggles and helpless woes. The
jury leaned forward with eyes fixed under the half-
hypnotic suggestion of his awful truth.

It was his second speech ; there was to be no

reply. He cleared the field. Not an opposing
argument stood erect when he was done. Men
wondered where he found his facts as well as his
eloquence. Surely he had been one of these men.
No; but by a woman's sympathy he had learned to
be one of them without passing through their very
trials. They had stood in the empty homes of
the poor too often not to know something of the
high crimes society commits against them. When
he described these poor men standing in the defense of their homes and babies, before the bull-
dogs of treacherous, unlicensed, and un-American
warfare, the judge looked up from the charge
which he was already writing, as though spellbound.

Elaine's eyes burned like coals of fire. It was
more than she had even dreamed he could do. In
a moment more it was over. A noise like swollen
waters breaking through a dam was heard, until
the judge's gavel fell. In stern tones he read the
charge, adding his own doubt of the officer's testimony, closing with the customary caution concerning the benefit of a doubt.

The jury retired. In four minutes they returned
and rendered their verdict, "Not guilty." No
power on earth could have stilled the storm. It
rose higher and higher. At first low, ominous;
then lighter, happier, louder, freer, until with
shouts the people bore the acquitted man, and his
brave defender on their brawny arms from the

court room. The judge and the prosecuting attorneys alone remained to congratulate the red-cheeked woman, who stood their peer in law, although not admitted to the rights of the bar. They did it unreservedly and heartily.

.   .   .   .

Tremont Temple is filled to its utmost capacity. The greatest pianist of the age is to be received by the musicians and the artists of Boston. Expectancy is at its highest. Who will do the honors of Boston? All eyes scan the program. Without exception a sigh of relief is heard. "Elaine Harley, the celebrated cornetist."

Her name divides the numbers of the program into two groups. As she appears the applause is greater, if possible, than when Europe's greatest artist bowed himself out for the third time a moment before. She has arranged a medley from Mendelssohn's "Songs Without Words," closing all with the Battle Hymn of the Republic.

Like delicate waves of ether, her first tones steal away the senses of men and women not accustomed to yield easily. A stillness like Lake Placid asleep before the storm, chained every listener. A shock in change of key, time and theme, sets every nerve twitching, to be followed by wailing anguish, tearful, tender pleading, every tone a sob. Then prayers of gratitude came, lifting the soul from its droopings upon sweeping wings of praise, and then, like a revelation of national glory, the Battle Hymn.

She has at last found the secret pitch of this American assembly. It trembles and sways, and swings; great beating waves surge to and fro. The People, the People—freedom, liberty. They rise with the closing strain, and sing it as one man. The proudest man in Boston that night was Maxwell Harley.

A DREAM.

July 13th, 1892, in a spirit of adventure, I built a pine-blazing fire on the very pinnacle of Cobble Hill. In a mystic sense it was the most dangerous and hazardous deed of my life. I little dreamed of the consequences; it was done in half-thoughtless bravado. The climbing had been circuitous and difficult. But the higher air was strangely revivifying. The vast mountain-riven horizon, spread like two great wings in either valley, until one's spirit mounted on them to an exultation expressible first in shouts, then in the desire for some new endeavor. What more novel than to send the cedars' blue smoke curling where for generations nothing but sun, air, and sound-waves had moved.

The tinder-dry pine was carried up by not very easy stages until the mirthful crackle and then the sheeted roar of the fire told how delighted were the imprisoned sun-sprites to be free, rushing frantically into the embracing air. But, alas! what other spirits had my rash exuberance set forth!

Wearied at last with the sport, and the sweeping spaces of vision whose only limits were the more distant mountains to the west, and Lake

Champlain in the east, I sought a shelter from the now noon-sun, and found it beneath the jutting pinnacle, in a half-concealed cave, whose shadows lay far back like hunted lives from the searching light. My "blue serge" coat folded over an age-rounded stone for a pillow, made my last wish as sleep came on, that this might be another Bethel.

And, indeed, how little we see with our eyes or hear with our ears! How the great unguessed mystery of the eternal and spiritual pulses unfelt all about our boastful senses when we wake! We say indifferently enough, "Here is life." The chemist laughs, and cries, "No, here is life, underneath all you saw." The biologist nervously plucks our mental sleeve, to suggest, half-hesitatingly: "No, here is life, deeper still. Not the molecule, but the atom, is the constituent unit." Then the metaphysician whispers, "Not so; organization is not life. The Infinite alone is life. Not things of sense are life, but a somewhat of activity by which things seen in multiform phenomena *seem* to be to the mind—this is life. The lump is not. The mind, acting and acted upon by mind, through phenomena, alone is." So away from things to entities I passed as I slept.

Then all at once I knew what awful consequences had followed my almost childish sport. I had with unwitting hands built the signal fire of the ancient Indian councils, calling from the unhappy hunting-ground the departed spirits of the

war-like but reverent Iroquois. The unpeopled
Adirondacks were in a moment as populous as is
the sea with waves. They seemed to come at first
not as individual chiefs and warriors, but in indis-
tinct groups of spirit. I soon understood this to
be the other world classification. Those similar
in nature had grown closer together, until so common were their tastes, desires and habits, it was
difficult to distinguish one from the other, or to be
sure of identity at all. But as a company of them
passed the wide front of my cave-couch, I saw that
waving about each spirit was an outline of gleaming light, closely resembling the electric flash
passing through a vacuum when the receiver is put
into contact with the opposite wires of an electric
battery. I thought at first these were physical
outlines, but I soon saw that it was merely the
suggestion of my own mental images of personality.

There was action of some high sort, but it
seemed more like a glowing thought than anything material. I knew then that the highest personality is not anthropomorphic, but intellectual,
emotional and willful, and that possibly the Greek
conception of God is truer than the Latin. (So
did I blend my waking dreams with this awful
vision).

Not long could I observe thus these new spiritual phenomena. In almost an instant nothing was
observable but the sadness of these myriad faces.

It seemed that it had become possible to so individualize emotion as to make it appear to be the whole person for the time. Each form seemed the personification of sadness. It was the strangest fascination I had ever experienced. No subtle hypnotism could resemble it. I yielded to it without an effort of resistance.

You have felt your throat beating with some awful sorrow, until you had to hold your hot hand against it lest you gasp for breath. Imagine one's whole nature to have come into such a condition. My eyes were not wet, for I seemed all tears. I knew nothing in the universe but that these souls were sad. I had swooned to all else.

Is this the heavenly sympathy? Had they cast it upon me like a strange spell? Will it ever come to be a condition of this poor, self-killed humanity here on earth? I hope it may. My throat seems bursting now with the memory of that awful consciousness of other hearts' woe. If a score of us could invoke it to abide, the world would be saved. Aye, if one. And has there not been One?

I listened at first for words. There were none. There was no need. Even in this life we never speak the best things; we communicate them. So now every glance, every motion, every posture was a communion with my outdrawn soul. I began to be conscious of their emotions without uttered speech. I knew they were inexpressibly sad, just

8

as I know even in this life that there is God.
Echoes of my own words came to me by and by.
But the echo, as happens when many walls return
the sound, was fuller, intenser by far, than the
original words. "Homeless," "Exiled," "Wan-
derer." Every pulse of their palpitating spirits
was a letter's sound. They were vibrant with
awful emotion.

It came to me at last, that there is but one
world. Life is continuous. It moves on in divers,
even diverse directions. It may reverse its tendencies—still, only one life.

I knew then the cause of this all-controlling
emotion. These cedar-fretted hills, these foaming
brooks, these rifted vales, this very signal-fire pinnacle of old Cobble, were of old, and are still, the
earth-holdings of these ancestors and their forbid-
den progeny. The woe of a race without a home,
groaning with the instinct to perpetuate itself, was
upon these restless spirits. Great desire was in
their eyes, such as Sarah must have known before
the angels' visit. A baffled purpose; a remembered hope—oh, the hopes which look back; and
a sighing energy. These were painfully plain.

Then a new consciousness came upon me instantly, just as when one stands in a tempest night,
lost, and a sudden, sweeping flood of lightning re-
veals his surroundings. As dreams turn in keyless
phantasmagoria, so now I knew I dreamed, and yet

separated myself from the dreamer long enough to see a real vision of my own time.

A vast, countless throng, hungry, restless, blindly toiling; cursing by their prayers, sometimes praying by their very curses; homeless, friendless; at war, not with their enemies, their foes were too shrewd for that; they made them murder each other, it made the number less, and in part satiated their frenzy for blood. The hills, the plains, the fields, the seas, all theirs, by every right of life or reason. Earning but not receiving, making but never owning, building but never dwelling within. Millers without flour, weavers without raiment, tillers without grain, diggers of coal without even the hearthstone, the fathers of babes without kisses, the lovers of God without a church. (Without a Christ? Let none blaspheme!) This is the life of the homeless, I thought. What shall be their future condition, if one may guess from the face of that noble chief who stood just at my side. Once proud, with uplift of head like a Homeric god, swift and dauntless. So broken now, as to draw pity from a slave. If what I have just described be the life of the homeless poor now, and this mountain vision be the condition into which we push them hereafter, what fate awaits those whose iron-handed greed pushes *les miserables* from their own into hell?

Then I lost all, even myself. I was a toiler. The rock split beneath my work-bent body as I arose. I hung suspended in the abyss. A voice came up on the vapors of the pit; ."Come, behold your masters." I laughed, I hissed, and with blood-bursting veins of demoniac glee, turned to look downward.

But the long-dwelling God-soul in me drove the passion out of me as I gazed with incalculable horror below. I wept, in spite of my cruel pain through the years, pitying tears into the yawning depths. Aye, I even prayed that my tears might quench the tormenting flames.

Then once more I was a dreamer on my stone bed, enwrapped with the Iroquois emotion. Beckoning to the bowed chieftain as he drew near, I looked into his eyes for a solution of a deeper mystery which my dream within a dream had suggested. I looked in vain for the fire-gleam, for the roving glance of distrust, and the quivering pupil of the crouching animal. On the earth, between days of chase and battle, there had been minutes in his life of moody sadness and prostration before the breathings of the Great Spirit. These minutes had grown into days now through the long processes of evolution. And through the ages still to come these drooping ones, doubtless, would lift their heads again with a new spirit and a new understanding. So does God right all wrong, so does he keep his compact with men signed into nature's bond.

But—and now dream turned philosophy—when shall man leave off damming up God's currents, compelling them to slowly wear their way through, when his real mission is to straighten and deepen the channels, even as John cried out in the wilderness?

Just now as we ruthlessly rob the poor and deprive them of their inheritance of the earth and its products, do we build the gold-dam of covetousness. But woe to us who build our palaces in the valley below! Comparably, Johnstown lay in the course of a mere mountain brook.

While I thought, a silence came about, as when one lifts the hands in prayer. I listened to, or rather felt, the circle of thought issuing from this untimely council which I would now have gladly disbanded and sent back beyond the clouds if I could have done so. But the signal had flamed from the mountain. It was too late. I felt that some awful event was impending. I dared not guess. I felt resolution rising like a mighty tide out of the dead calm of their sadness. It rose with no lashing lines on its crest. Not for revenge, not for recovery, not for self at all. The old conditions had been left behind too long for these. Something better, more indomitable, winning. I knew it as soon as they. I shuddered for the immediate consequences of it; I rejoiced over the inevitable end. I seemed to be impressed with their own will, as I lay scarce daring to breathe.

" We are spirits of nature. We loved our mother, her hills, and stars, and sun-filled stalks and pods. We loved to be close to her bosom. We believed the simple lodge of the forest was better than the gilded mansion of our pale-faced brother. We still believe it. Our summit of vision beyond the earth-life has confirmed our faith, ignorant and physical as were our conceptions then. Great cities, mighty structures, vast wealth parcelled out, or kept with joint-stiffened clutch, commercial billions, are not civilization, are not progress, are not life, are not happiness, are not God-winning! They curse!

" We know well how spirit guides spirit, though hindered by flesh. We, here by Mt. Cobble's signal flame, holy as was our Israel fathers' Carmel-fire, solemnly covenant with the Great Spirit, Jehovah Father, and with one another, that each shall choose for himself one of earth's bravest, most heroic souls, and shall be to it a constant fellowship, whispering our nature and God-given secret into its innermost heart, until the nations shall learn that happiness, fraternity and eternal life alone are found close to nature, and, in that which we have since learned on yonder high plains—peace."

I groaned with the thought of revolution. But I exulted in hope of evolution. I saw it all, though it shook my soul to the very arms of death. I lived on the border of two conditions for an hour, with awful indecision⸴ ⸳ To enter that and take on new activities, or remain in this, and help turn the stony face of humanity back to the morning. Can it turn? Is there any morning? Instinct answers: "Back to nature." The Christ answers: "Up to peace." And now abideth these three: faith, hope, and fraternity, but the greatest of these is Fraternity.

There are ashes on Cobble Hill, but is there not a flame in your soul, my brother?

JIM'S VICT'RY.

THE last, bright-tinted leaves had turned brown and ugly, and their number was growing less and less upon the more hardy stems of the birch and maple boughs of the Adirondack forest-home of one who shall be nameless here, as he was nameless always by reason of excessive modesty except to a small circle of friends who knew him simply because they lived near him, and were often in want. The nearly bare branches, and the swaying, slender, sapling trees, standing erect and defiant, as youthful conceit ever does, not recognizing that the great-hearted trees generations old about them alone kept them from snapping in the first stiff gale, and the wind-stirred leaves on the acorn-covered ground made music to all ears but his, very unlike that of spring, when the first green leaves and sprouting stems sing sprightly in the warming winds.

To all, this music of autumn was wild and uncanny, such as they thought accompanied disembodied spirits when at night they prowl forth from their dust-dry graves in quest of an abode where the worm cometh not. In their homes at night these superstitious people shivered and paled in spite of loud laughter, as the gusty wind swooped down from its perch on the highest trees, down through the seared leaves still hanging there in spite of their fate, and dancing with many a whirl in the rustling leaves on the ground. It never sobered them, however; it merely drove them farther within, and made them seek for amusement and dissipation, and forgetfulness of their half-stirred consciences.

Thus the men, while the women, the wives and daughters of these ignorant foresters, sad eyed and lonely, sat apart from the glee and sparkling glass, not conscious of wrong deeds or thoughts, but feeling with a woman's deep intuition that something was wrong, yet not knowing how to remedy it. To them the autumn winds seemed like voices from the great unknown world of which they had some faint conception, ignorant as they were, and to which they sometimes offered feeble prayers in their distress. To the mother it seemed like the last wail of her sick babe when it fretted with pain in her arms, and struggling, at last died, long before she knew it was in danger; when she had held it for hours alone, so cold that its icy hands seemed no less warm than when in health it had toyed with her fingers.

To the shy, almost speechless girl, just budding into fair womanhood, the autumn wind in the long evening, as she sat back in the shadows cast by the flickering flames of the wide fire-place, was like the last words of her lover, when one morning he hurriedly left her in company with a band of friends who were bent on seeing the new city springing up into prominence some fifty miles away. She felt a dreary presentiment that she should never see him again, and his words, "Good bye, Prue," she could hear over and over again in the sobbing wind.

But he of whom we write this story heard in the wind no such gloom and misery, nor did he ever need stimulant of any sort to drive away its presence.

To him, it sang the same song that the spring sang, in the same key, the same theme; that was the major, this the minor, and of the two he loved the minor more. The one was bright and rejoicing over life and health, which had come, in bud and flower and beauty; the other was a song of trust to him, rather than fear. It seemed to say : "The summer is gone, the flowers are dead, but the soul is still alive, and its God is about it, and warming it evermore. Nature may blight, the earth grow cold, the stars go out and the sun lose its radiance, this body perish as does the leaf, but God liveth still, endlessly." It told him that under all these dead leaves and in every black stem were germs of life, now hidden, waiting for the springtime. That life never dies, no winter kills it; the soul is life; life is God.

But there is a story. This lover of nature lived far more out in the field than he did within his comfortable house, even in winter, for he found crystals from heaven on the earth, helpless twigs held by a load of ice which he could remove, lame rabbits and limping birds to call his attention and care. He had lived in this same spot forty years.

No one knew whence he came. His hair was already white with the frosts and snowfalls of sixty winters. The lines on his peculiar face were many and deep, but not such as fear or doubt make, nor remorse; rather, the lines of thought and care.

His wealth consisted in the increased value of his land by improvement, chiefly by his own hands, and such little accumulation of valuable stores as naturally comes to one long busy in the same place. His, the only well kept fences, the only trimmed trees, the only repaired house and barns, and, above all, his the only flower gardens in all that community. To these, visitors often came from the little town, springing up some miles away. The mail stage, on its weekly journey staid rarely enough anywhere else than before the wide gate of this primitive home. But its burden was always much lighter after stopping here. So regular were its visits that a rude watering-trough had been constructed by the huge gate post, and always contained fresh water on the morning of the stage's expected arrival.

In this ripe autumn time it was, as the hermit

lover of nature stood ready to receive his mail one
Friday morning, that the driver, as he whipped
his horses up to the trough, upon reaching back
for the mail-bag, asked hurriedly, who lived in the
log-house a quarter of a mile back, at the turn in the
road. "Jim Allison," replied Mr. Armile—thus we
shall name him—"Every one calls Allison, Jim."
"Guess they're in trouble, the old woman come
a-runnin' out as I passed, with her apron up to her
face and asked me as I would please to tell you to
come up, that Jim had 'em agin. I told her as
that I would, and she bellered louder than ever.
Snaked if I see whar the boys git the stuff out
here. I'll be swigged if ever I bringed 'em any."
Mr. Armile looked as if he had some doubt about
this assertion.

The cloud deepened upon his face as he said,
half to himself: "I had some hope of him this
time. But I told him this was the last; once
more, and I must let him go on his way forever.
Too long now have I held him up without hope.
But then I did have faith this time. He talked
differently; something unusual must have happened."

"Well, I guess there were," said the stage driver,
while he put up the reins of the now satisfied
horses, "from what that black dwarf down at
the creek said."

"Who was that? Joe Dives?" "'Pears to me
he did call himself Dives or somethin' of the kind."

" If he is here it is easy to account for the other, for his heart is blacker than his face, and his soul more bent than his ugly body."

" Well, as to that I am not able to testify; but least-ways he said as how there was trouble ahead for somebody, and wanted to know if he could ride with me to the 'line,' and I told him he could for a dollar. He asked if I still druv by your place. I told him I guessed there wouldn't be much use for me through here if I didn't. Said he'd see a friend and overtake me at the cross-roads if he decided to go, and for me to rest here as long as I could."

Turning quickly toward the driver as the thought flashed upon him what to do, Mr. Armile asked: "You have an official commission, have you not, to arrest anyone who may molest you, or seem suspicious, on your route?"

" Yes-sir-ee; only last week I tuk a fellar to Princeton to jail for skulkin' along inside the fence, and lookin' kinder dangerous."

" Well, I want you to drive over and arrest the dwarf, for he will be at the cross roads; of that I am sure. Take him with you to Princeton and hand him over to the sheriff with this note. He will be wanted there, I can assure you, and I will be responsible for the part I ask you to do. He is guilty of enough crimes to jail him for life, and we have sufficient proofs."

The driver drove on at a good jolt, glad of a chance to show his authority.

Mr. Armile hurried down the road towards the humble home of him whom his mother in her quaint way had said to be in a drunken fit. He muttered as he walked: "If I can only get the dwarf out of here forever, I can save half of these men. Of course they are worth saving. A broken-winged bird, fluttering on the ground, its shining eyes bursting from its little head in its fright, is worth saving; even a flower, half broken by the dashing rain, ought to have a friendly hand and a prop. Surely a man, a prince in this world of nature, the highest of all life on the earth— more than that, given a promise by his Creator that this life is not cut off, but goes on forever— surely he, when broken-winged or bent by the storm, needs a hand and a prop! Maybe my hand can help this poor fellow; if only he will lean on the support the Good Father gives us all."

At the close of these meditations he found himself at the bend in the road, and in sight of Allison's log house—a home rough in exterior, and not much better within, with bare floor and walls, and scant furniture. But it had been the field of as hard battles as ever were fought on the earth. For there is no conflict like that between appetite for strong drink and a man's desire to be worthy and to conquer. It had been an equal combat up to this time. Jim's home, his aged mother, his three motherless babies, his desire to be respectable, the friendship of Mr. Armile, and a very faint idea of God taught by this one great-hearted man, who now crossed his wretched household—these on one side; and ignorance, superstition, an aimless life, love of sport, whisky, Joe Dives the black dwarf, and Hell, on the other side. In the last battle these had won, and the defeat was shameful.

On the hard couch in the dimly-lighted room lay the poor fellow with his face to the wall. Over him his aged mother had thrown an old coat which had served through many winters; it seemed to cling to him as though some sort of affection had grown up between them in all those years of mutual hardship.

As the visitor entered, he tiptoed across the creaking floor, hat in hand, and sat upon the low stool beside the couch. He laid his strong hand upon the shoulder of the sleeper. He moved under it, and turning slightly saw who it was, when, with a groan he turned back again.

"Jim, my boy," came the warm, mellow voice of the forest hermit, "I am sorry to see you down here. How did it all happen, the old story again I fear?" Then the weak man turned toward the speaker as if to say something.

"Not now, Jim, you are not fit to talk now. Wait until to-morrow and then we will talk it all over."

"But, sir," began the man with quivering lips.

"No, not a word now, no more rash promises. We can fix it up to-morrow, if it isn't too late.

Jim, Jim!" he almost sobbed, losing for a
moment his self-control, for so long had he loved
these poor men of his community, all whipped by
appetite as they were, that his heart was as soft
as a child's. Rough to look upon, almost stern in
his words, nevertheless his soul was sweetly tuned
to nature's music, and little children loved him
more than their own fathers.

In the meanwhile the old mother had gone out
to take the children to Mr. Armile's for something
to eat, and to be away from the scene, by his own
command.

With a sad shake of his head, and placing his
hand on the cot, he bent over that he might the
more closely observe the face of the man and see
how deep his intoxication had been, for somehow
he seemed to be unlike himself.   There was a
nervous twitching, a restlessness never before
noticed in him when recovering from his stupor.

No sooner had he done speaking, than Jim
seized his hand in his, fairly raising himself up
on his other arm, his eyes burning like coals of
fire through the shadows in the room, and cried
out: "Hear me, hear me, for God's sake! It is
not whiskey—can't you see? I am not drunk. I
have kept my word to you. It has cost me my
life," he gasped. "I didn't dare tell mother, nor
the babies, but I am stabbed. All night my life-
blood has been dripping away, drop at a time. I
just prayed one prayer. Let me live until the

only man in the world who loves me and has
saved me, can get here, and know why I am
dying. Now you are here. I tried to speak when
you first came in, but my tongue seemed stiff. But
your sad face let it loose. You thought I had fall-
len again. I would not have died for all of that
heaven you talk about, and had you believe me
drunk. I feel strong with you here. If it was not
for the great, wet blood-pool under my side I believe I might get up. It sickens me. I know it is
too late now, but I can tell you how it was."

Slowly he told the story: "Late last night I
heard a rap at the door, and when I opened it the
black dwarf came hobbling in. You know how
we hate him, you and I; we have cause to, for he
has robbed me of everything. He seemed fierce,
and before he had stood long in front of the fire
there, he asked for a drink of whisky. I told him
I had none in the house, that I had reformed.
With a sneer on his face which must be like that
of the damned, he hissed between his teeth. I
was determined he should not disturb me. He
gave me the lie twice, but I kept my temper. He
was raving by this time, and swore he would have
a drink or he would burn me out. Just then Nellie came up to me for something, and before I
could see or think he had her by her little thin
arms, shaking her till she lost her breath.

"'Tell me, you little white-faced witch, where
the whisky is. Tell me, or I'll kill you.'
9

"She looked like an angel, sir. She never trembled or nothing, but looked straight at him. She was always afraid of him before. She said: ' My father don't drink any more since Mr. Armile—' and, sir, your name seemed to make him crazy, for he lifted her in his little iron arms, and whirled with her toward the blazing fire-place. Like the wind I was at his side and undid his hands, and carried her, sobbing, to the cot here, and as I bent over to lay her down, wondering what I should do with the wretch, I felt something in my side, first cold, and I shivered, then hot, and I fairly burned with fever. I fell beside the child, while he escaped through the door. She put her arms about me and said, ' Father, are you hurt?' I told her no, that I felt a little sick, and would rest awhile. Soon mother come in from the neighbor's with the other children. I told them I was not well, but all the while I could feel the hot blood settling about my flesh. And this morning when I looked at Nellie's hands I saw blood on one of them. Her father's blood, made by whisky! Child of woe! Oh, the night, the blood!"

Mr. Armile saw that the fever was raging high now, and that the poor man's brain was crazed. He checked him, and keeping down the great, choking sobs that would swell up in his throat in spite of himself, he took the dying man's hand, and soothed him as best he could.

He grew calmer soon, but was so weak he could

only pant; he had outdone himself. "Tell me the
story you told me one day," he whispered, "out in
the great woods. You had a flower; it was losing
its leaves; you said it was dying for others like
itself, but Jesus died for men who hated Him.
Tell me again. I never hated Him, but I didn't
know Him. I knew you, I loved you, I did what
you told me; and now, tell me, where will I be,
and who will be there?"

"Yes," said the great man of nature, "I told
you of the flower. It died when its time came to
drop its seed. But Jesus, who loved men more
than I have loved you, was nailed to the death-
tree until He died. His great heart broke, Jim,
broke. He shed His blood; you have shed yours
for your Nellie, and for all these neighbors of
yours, for they will curse whiskey forever when
they stand at your grave. But these were your
companions. Jesus shed His blood for the very
men who murdered Him. He spreads His hands
above every head that bows in the whole world.

"You have fought a noble fight, the best I ever
knew. You had nobody but me to hold you up,
but you fought it through. It has cost you your
life here, but, Jim, not your life up yonder."

"Will the flower live again?" he whispered.

"I believe so, Jim, but I know you will, and
forever."

"Yes, yes," murmured the fast-dying man.
"Bessie,—she died last year,—for me,—when I

was mad with whisky; she will be there; Bessie, —I married her,—almost a girl; she did her best. 'Pears to me—I hear her; Bessie,—Bessie,—is— that you?"

And clutching the great brown hand of his only friend on earth, he shivered and died. His body was ice, but on his face played a smile as warm as a sunbeam and so peaceful that when his old comrade looked upon his face at the grave, he said aloud: "Jim whipped that time; I can see the smile of vict'ry on his face."

Twenty strong men, with wet eyes and shaky hands, put their mark over their names as Mr. Armile wrote them under the pledge, beside that new grave.

So in a forsaken region, with no church, no teacher, scarcely a Bible within its borders, twenty-one ignorant, careless men were saved from awful death by one man.

Long did Mr. Armile stand out in the open field, the night after the burial. He felt not the increasing chill in the night air, but leaning against a kingly hemlock, he looked up through its moving branches at a bright star in the measureless space above. The swaying boughs moved to and fro as if trying to hide the star from him, but always he saw it. So it seemed, our sorrows, our woes, our very sins, swing between us and the Christ, as if trying to hide Him from us, but always through them all we see Him still, brighter and brighter.

In the warm southern room of his own home that night, the autumn winds sang three motherless, fatherless babies to sleep. Fatherless no more, for the great Father had given them a guardian, and that guardian, the lover of the stars, and the great nature-world around him, soon after fell into happy sleep, while the wind, like some great winged angel of glory from the distant mountains, and as if guarding him, sang all the night long, "Peace, peace, everlasting peace."

"AUNT MODGIE."

It happens, now and then, that where one least expects it, is to be found the most beautiful bit of scenery, in both nature and humanity.

Not far from Cedar Rapids, as one climbs unadorned hills and is satiated with unchanging fields, he suddenly looks from a hill summit down upon as beautiful a valley as the sun ever shone into. Especially is this beauty remarkable if it be looked upon in the month when the gold begins to gleam on the green of the grain and the meadow.

Strange that in prosaic Iowa a gem from poetic Italy should have hid itself through all these years, a stranger from its nature-loved home, where the skies are never brazen, nor the climate cruel.

The depth of this valley is almost cavernous. The shadows of the great hills round about fall into it like the presence of slumbering giants, while the shifting lights and shades on the hills themselves are full of motion, made by the turning leaves—now dark green, now lighter, as the winds reverse them; or still more marked by the overshadowing sweep of some pilgrim cloud, which, straying from a great cloud convention in the West,

(134)

dares to brave the sun all alone, eclipsing it section by section.

A path winds in from the main road, and follows the curve of the brook until it is lost in the broad porch which alone marks the front of an old brick house. Its one story and a half took on shape some half century ago, when, doubtless, its magnificent pile of brick and walnut stood as a monument of pride and " bigishness," in the eyes of envious neighbors, who were wont to say their unselfish prayers beneath the "clapboard" roofs of palaces, whose strength was the heart of their oak logs. An ugly house, and standing out upon a plain of sand and weeds, would have no suggestion of home-likeness; but in the center of this valley, it seemed also the center of life, about which all these moving beauties of brook, and path, and hill, and leafy tree, revolved.

The red bricks sent their color thrill far out into the shadows and the subdued colors of the valley, until it came to be at last like the song a great singer sings, which animates all the silent ones, until to the listener every one seems to sing, even himself. So, this bit of red colored with a living glow all the somber darkness of its surroundings. Thus that which alone would be unattractive, when fulfilling its mission, in its place, grew strangely beautiful. Has this no analogy in the life which is human ?

One would expect, under the spell of this valley's

charms, an ideal life must be found. Happy the
controlling life which rules in the old red house,
moulded day after day by the influence of the
mystic hills! Surely, thinks the poet, to look up
to those towering summits morning and night,
wondering what lies beyond them, studying their
whisperings and sighings, or their moody silence—
surely, a perfect life might find the end of its
development here.

But let us see. We will follow the path, and
resisting the whispered entreaties of the rippling
brook, continue, until we near the house undiscovered.

"Saliny, Saliny," wails a peevish voice, heard
distinctly through the open window; "where are
ye? You do beat all to git away where no one
can find ye: come here." No answer.

"I'll be bound she's gone down to that brook
agin; I never seed sich a gal. These yer four walls
is no home fer her, no more than if they want
here; deed, I do believe she wishes they were
pulled down. The pesky woods and hills are *her*
home. If it want for me she would never come
home except to sleep. It *is* kinder hard for the
poor thing to hev to wait on me so much, but sick
folks is sick folks, and ye hev to wait on them or
they'll die, and if I don't git helped in a minute,
die I shall; Saliny!"

"Yes, I'm coming."

"Ye are always comin', I wish ye'd git here

once in a while; my back is nearly broke in two, layin' here waitin' to be turned; now do be easy."

She was easy; not by reason of a strong form, or well developed muscle, but because of that grace and skill which so often accompany the lithe and delicate body. She wasted no strength, made no awkward movements; there was no half-lifting, and then a sudden laying down for a renewal of strength. She knew just how to lift the almost helpless body of "Aunt Modgie," as she always called her. Not a very appropriate name, to be sure; but the one she had lived by, and she said it was "good enough to die by."

They were in no way related, these two women. The younger had been adopted by the elder, when she was four years old, out of an Orphans' Home, in the city near by, "for better or for worse," as she said, when she took her, mistaking the occasion, doubtless, for the one she in her lonely spinsterhood had long been secretly longing for. But that was not to be; in the glory and strength of her youth she had loved with her whole heart, but her hero had gone away without a word of warning, and she had never again seen him. For a long time she had waited, looking down this same winding path. Often in the shadows of evening she thought she saw his familiar form, and often she awoke from her dreams with his step ringing in her ears.

She and her brother had kept the little valley

place, until at last he had died. She had hardly
righted the house after the funeral, until she had
determined what to do. "I cannot live alone—I
could live *all* alone, but I am not alone now any
more; some one is always near me. But I am a
hundred times lonesomer than if he was not always
comin' back to me. I must have some one here
who will take up my attention. No one of my
own age can do that; nothin' will do it but a sick
person, or a baby. They say the 'sylum is very
full this season. I believe I will look 'em over. I
would ruther have a sickly one if only it wouldn't
die ; but I'll see."

Her untrained mother-heart sobbed, and sobbed again, as she looked upon that multitude
of motherless waifs at the asylum, cared for by
the matrons of the home, but motherless still. No
great thrill of child-life would ever set their hearts
quivering with affection. So soon they must make
way for others and step out into what paths, what
ways, into what struggles, what destinies! She
silently wept as she thought of it.

She wanted to take half a dozen of the puniest
and palest ones, and had nearly decided to do so,
when the fierce pain in her breast, stinging for a
moment, repeated its old warning. She might be
more helpless than they before many years, and
she ought not to make so many lives dependent
upon her without being able to carry them
through.

As she looked, a little, frail thing, in the arms of an older child, let its nodding head fall back against the bosom of its little nurse. The day was warm, and it had been too severe a trial to bring it from its half-finished sleep. She had noticed its eyes fixed upon her when first she had entered, and had instantly felt drawn towards it. Some familiar look, some half-forgotten, nameless wistfulness in its eyes, seemed to speak to her, until her heart had been stirred, as we have seen, to be a mother to all these waifs if only she might be able.

"Let me take her and rest you," she said to the child, who gladly gave her up from her aching arms. "How light she is, poor thing! Are her parents both dead?"

"We think so," replied the matron; "we know her mother to be dead. Her father came with her here, and said he would return, but he has never done so. He looked very strange-like, and seemed rather unsettled in his mind. He was very poor, and looked like he had eaten nothing for two or three days. The child has his eyes, with the same wistful look in them."

"Did you see the mother?" she asked.

"We only saw her in her coffin," said the matron. "She was large, and rather coarse-featured, with the mouth firmly set. They say her hands were clinched when she died, and no one could open them. The child had this little locket

and chain about her neck when she was brought
here. In it is a picture of her father."

"May I see it?" She half dreaded to look at it
for some reason, but she opened it bravely. Sure
enough, the presentiment which had swept over
her a moment before was verified. She had worn
the locket many a time herself. It was the face of
him who had gone from her, but kept coming back
to her memory and in her dreams.

She understood it all now. He had spoken once
of a woman whom he had met in his boyhood,
who held a strange spell over him. He told her
he had vowed never to see her again. She knew
now that he had seen her again; that she had·
followed him, and he had at last given up the
struggle and gone with her in spite of his nobler
love. She had married him, and this was their
child. The mother was dead, perhaps the father.
The child was unmistakably like its father. She
must take it, and in her love for it, hide some of
her awful pain, for the wound was throbbing
again and breaking under this new pressure.

So home with her, and close in her arms all the
way, had gone the baby with the beautiful eyes.
Through the years these two lives had come up higher and higher, almost out of the valley to the very
hills. The child lost its frailness and pallor, and
took on the glow and strength of the woods and
the flowers. Her voice was tuned to the music of
the birds and brook.

Yet there were discords and surprises. The
child caught a certain waywardness from nature;
stormy, moody, almost violent at times; but love
and tenderness always soothed her, and when her
returning calmness re-assumed control, she fled
always to the hills for penitence, not returning
until the smiles played through her tears, as the
refreshed flowers after a heavy rain nod beneath
their pearly crowns.

She was loyal to "Aunt Modgie," and shirked no
duty which love could prompt.

On the other hand, as great changes had come
upon "Aunt Modgie." The pain had come and gone,
until she had begun to expect it at regular inter-
vals. At last, after a sharp attack of lung fever,
during one long-remembered, damp winter, it came
to stay. Her very voice grew hollow with the sound
of disease. The hands, once so soothing, were nervous and quick, and seemed sometimes almost to
sting when they meant to caress. Where it had
been her wont to entreat Salina—for she had christened her thus at adoption—she now commanded.
This had come about gradually, just as the helplessness had grown, scarcely perceptibly.

But the stoop in Salina's shoulders was more
marked, while an old look of many years had
come into her eyes.

The hills and the brook were still her delight,
and at times her only comfort. The ravine that
led from the brook up into the hills seemed now,

more and more, like an entrance into the presence
of the Infinite, and in those long, silent commun-
ions she found a gracious strength.

Struggles like the battles of armed hosts, equal
in strength and number, came to those two lonely
women. The one with the dreams of youth full
upon her, longing to see the great world, half
doubting sometimes between it and her afflicted
benefactor; for this her only home was, she knew,
the gift of this lonely woman. To the elder, in
the impatience of pain and unrest, came the old
fight. Was God merciful? So long had she
waited, so hard had she tried to forget the father
in the child, and yet felt· the defeat, as only her
aching heart could know! To-day she had determined Salina should know the story of her birth,
and their relation to each other. The peevishness
with which she summoned her upon the morning
of which this story speaks was by no loss of love,
but because of the nervousness and weakness of
one who, though long sick, undertakes a great task.

"Come closer to me, dear, I hev somethin' to
tell you. I do this because I feel the mornin' is
dawnin' over the hills at last, and the shadows of
the valley are a-liftin'. Now you must not say a
word until I am done. Take this little locket;
you have wondered why I looked at it so often,
oftener than you did, even. But I hev never looked
at it without lookin' at you, too. There is a great
secret here, and you must know it. Saliny, my

child, these eyes of your father's, so like your own, were *mine* once, and were like the stars of the night to one lost. They looked down into my soul, and I loved him. No, wait a moment; I want to tell you all."

Then she told her all she knew of his life, his temptation and weakness, and how she hoped that he still lived.

"Oh, Aunt Modgie," Salina sobbed, as she clung to her, "why did you not tell me years ago? Oh, the bitter words I have said to you, the many times I have neglected you, and your heart so full of pain! How can I live and know you have suffered so much, and that I might have helped you infinitely more than I did?"

"Be still, child, you know not what you say. Between the storms of my life there hev been calms without number, hours when I was positively happy a-carin' for you. Long ago I would hev died, had it not been for you, and died, Saliny, worst of all, a-hatin' God; but you hev carried me to the hills yonder so often, that I found the great heart of the Father at last, and it's all like a sea, Saliny, a mighty sea of peace. I'm lookin' for the dawn yonder. See, its faint glimmerin's a-peepin' over the old hills in the east! The day is a'most here. I must sleep once more, and then I will not be tired when the day comes. Wake me when the night is all gone. Just one word, dear child—

find your father, if he is alive; save him as you
have me; he needs you."

Long into the morning the feverish young
woman, now so pitifully undone, lay with her head
on the bed, with one hand outstretched, groping
now and then for the fingers that each time she
felt them, grew colder and stiffer. Once they
stirred with a quivering of the body, in which a
whisper seemed to be half formed—"the dawn,
the mornin' "—and then the night was all gone.

By some strange volition, the morning of the
next day a stranger came slowly up the path to
the house. He was stooped and gray; his face
curved with pain and wistful longing. From his
eyes all the hope had gone out long ago. Came,
he knew not why, unless it was to look at the old
brick house once more,—and die, for his life had
been a struggle without end, without hope. He
had no thought of going in; no thought of being
recognized, for the face of the man was not like the
face in the locket; by days of sorrow, penitence
and age his old strength and beauty were almost
gone.

But there was crape on the door, the scent of
heliotrope came through the open windows, and a
silence held the place like that which death alone
makes.

He scarcely knew what he did. He was in the
room in an instant; for the first time in all the
long years since they parted, he wept. Such tears

as no mother ever weeps over her dead boy, or a child over a mother's death-face; tears of heart's love and heart's pain distilled through years of sorrow and care for this one hour.

If his face told not the secret, his tears did; and told it to her who alone was watching with her dead. She waited, half alarmed, until the first burst of grief was over, then throwing her arms about his neck, she pressed her lips to his wrinkled forehead and almost sobbed into his ears, "Father, father, I have loved her, too, ever since she took me, a baby, to be her own."

Too sacred for utterance are some heart-communions—such were these. The father had never expected to see her again. To him she had been the scar of his weakness and almost crime. But now he was sanctified by the love of these two women, the living dead, the dead alive, both of whom he had wronged.

The clinging girl had his heart instantly. She gave new life to him, and healed his wounded spirit, revived his dead faith in God, and set flowing again the currents of a life long stagnant, more powerful in its energies, more wonderful in its strength to do good to men by reason of its weakness and cross. Together they prospered; fed, clothed, and made homes for hundreds of poor waifs.

Father and daughter, victims of error, restored

10

by tears and suffering, came into a saving fellowship with men on earth, and into a blessed immortality.

JOHN BROWN.

(WRITTEN AT JOHN BROWN'S GRAVE IN THE ADIRONDACKS,
JULY 17TH, 1892.)

ÆONED MARCY holds no firmer place along the silent
    Adirondack guard
Than Thou, rough-hewn old Chieftain, 'mong those
    who for liberty have dared.

Thy dust, rock-held by Placid's copious deeps with
    songs of pines for requiem of state,
Is no securer kept, than in the hearts of patriots, thy
    valors great.

Here amid thy farmer friends thou taughtst the
    weakling grain 'twixt bruising rocks to grow;—
The teacher since of weakling souls, o'er-topping
    Fate, their powers to know.

Thou clay-marked son of earth, I wonder what divine
    emanations filled thy toil-bent form,
Till riding over hatreds dire, like fire-charged, cleans-
    ing storm,

Foes like forests fell; and dammed up streams of
    ancient, stagnant, love of self were burst,
And love of men, aye, slaved and famished men, and
    suff'ring Christ were first.

*   *   *   *   *   *   *   *

Oh, Pentecostal Christ, quick-wing another dauntless
    soul to storm the citadel of caste,
Till *slaves* and *kings* of Toil alike the Patmos dream
    shall see at last.

(147)

A DOUBLE REVELATION.

"Is THAT really a tally-ho?"

"Well, it has that appearance; part tally-ho, part horse; six of one and half a dozen—"

"How in the wide world does one get up?"

"You will find the world wider than you have dreamed when once you are up and going. So very wide, I fear that you may try to fill two places at the same time with that sprightly little body of yours."

"No matter. I shall have one tally-ho lark if I occupy three places at one time."

It was at Westport. It was their first experience with mountains. Like the amateur tourists they were, they had decided to follow the guide-book, simply because there was nothing else to follow. They bought their tickets to Westport, and not somewhere else, for the sole reason that "it was the entrance to the gateway of the Adirondacks." Adrian Winake had been a college man through four or five indifferent years, at a quiet western school, with a diversified record between the extremes of "remarkable brilliancy," and "logging," a western term for "playing" the professors.

(148)

He had learned one valuable lesson not in the text: To assume knowledge where the effort is not too great, and the ends to be gained considerable. Hence his wise remark upon the tally-ho. The effort of saying it was not great, the end to be gained, to make a passing impression upon this rather vivacious young lady, his friend's sister, who had been entrusted to his care as far as Elizabethtown. Here Holwell Berkeley would join them within a week from New York, having prolonged his stay there in business engagements.

Leona Berkeley was a typical young western girl. She was full of curiosity, a bright, quizzical, healthy curiosity, not the common sort, inherited from abandoned paradise. Generous, sometimes to indiscretion, wholly and almost absurdly innocent. A little knowledge of Greek and Analytics had given her, she imagined, keys to every closed door of intellectual attainment. She was not slow to try them, either. A few had proved rusty and rebellious. She had not found fault with her keys, however. Withal, an entertaining, thoroughly good young lady, and with a much wider horizon than one would have at first supposed. That one is much concerned about the pebbles or flowers at his feet, does not always indicate that he has not discovered any heights, or looked far, this way and that.

Full of chatter about little things, of quick repartee and smiles, assuming innocence for effect,

half pouting when you took her too seriously,
gently kind to your faults, and soothing to your
little heart-aches, confidential, but with an inviolable reserve when she imagined you were becoming too sentimental—such a wide-awake sight-seer
was Leona Berkeley.

She took in everthing rapidly, vividly. No
kodak's delicate film ever took or held quicker or
more natural impressions of the sunlit world. She
caught the edges of things. The striking, the particular, was always pleasing or alarming her.
Winake had noted the depot, the hurrying crowd,
the distant, first slopes of the hills, all in one
sweeping glance. She saw only the idol of her
dreams for weeks—the tally-ho with its six creamy
horses. Trunk checks, inquiries as to route, time
of destination,—these might concern more sordid
minds, but the top of the coach was her ultima
thule. She fairly clapped her hands, unmindful
of the attention she drew, when, having climbed
the stumpy little ladder, she sat perched upon the
last and highest seat.

The first range of hills set her wild, not by their
loftiness, for they were not very high, but by their
outline, their depths of green and encircling nearness. Changing her mood, she grew dreamy,
almost sad, when looking back, she saw the glistening waves of Lake Champlain and the mist-
darkened Green Mountains beyond. She was getting her first impressions of new space relations.

Her emotion is a common one. The desire to be at some hazily distant cliff or peak, the impulse to start at once,—it cannot be far, you think,—then the baffling after-thought of the miles of wearying way, indeed the utter impossibility of attaining it; a whole life of yearning and struggle and surren- der, has its miniature in that first emotion spring- ing from the mountain horizon.

When at last the eight miles between Westport and Elizabethtown were nearly finished, and she had shouted question after question down to the rather reticent driver, Raven Hill, with its black wings darker than ever. just then under a raven cloud-shadow, loomed up before her, and then further on, emerging from a sinuous alder-sheltered mile, she saw Pleasant Valley spreading like a lit- tle world before them, river, fields of daisies and grain, village and all, this prairie-visioned girl, for the first time since she had left New York City, was speechless.

"Elizabethtown!" shouted the driver with a crack of the whip, as the coach rolled down and around the declining slopes, thundering across the bridge of songful little Bouquet River, halting with a grand flourish at the post-office in the valley.

"*When, pray*, do they find time to read letters, much less write them here? I wouldn't want to be disturbed, not even by the shortest telegram."

"Suppose Holwell should be prevented from

meeting us here, you would want to know—"

"Stop, Mr. Winake. I won't even think anything that is in discord with this place."

" Don't you suppose people ever sin or die here ? Didn't you notice the graveyard a mile or so back ?"

" When did you take your Bachelor of Divinity degree ? Don't preach. "

" Ah, there is a church on the hill. Had we not better turn back ?"

" I do wonder what need they have for churches here. I should think every hill would be a ser-mon."

" Wouldn't they be rather rocky ?"

" Mr. Winake, I shall walk up this hill and alone, if you do that again. I am ashamed of you, positively ! Slang in the Adirondacks !"

" What in the Sam Hill are ye drivin' so fast fer, Tom ? Don't yer see yer critters is about to drap ? " came up from the street.

Adrian made a gesture towards her as though expecting her to faint. " You must get used to it, Miss Berkeley. I know it's a sudden shock. I have passed through it myself. I once visited Concord, and standing with bated breath—bated is good—at the very door of Emerson's home, I heard an Irishman swear like a trooper. Metaphor-ically I carried myself out for interment. I ven-ture that you will find that a majority of the poets, novelists, and 'lovers of nature,' as you would

say in the Adirondacks, are summer boarders.
The average of the natives will run about as it
does the world over. But look yonder! Can I believe my eyes, or rather can you believe them?
There is a jail, and a court-house! Can it be possible they need wardens and lawyers in such an
environment?"

"I believe you expect to study law next year,
Mr. Winake."

"Well, why?"

"Oh, nothing, only I thought you spoke of them
as a sort of associated evil with jails and wardens."

"The Windsor House."

"A waltz, Miss Berkeley, in the drawing-room!
Better try some other house, hadn't we?" said
Winake with a teasing twinkle in his genial eyes.

"If you say another word I shall be vexed. Of
course, I knew that people ate and drank and slept,
and even danced right in the very eyes of old
White Face—it must be near here somewhere;
where is the guide-book? But I think you might
let me indulge in a little imagination when you
know I—"

"I beg your pardon, Miss Leona; but I only
wanted to prepare you for the unpoetic side of life,
even in Pleasant Valley. I may be over-inclined
to see that side of it. But I couldn't help observing, as we came, that the meadows are nine parts
white and yellow daisies to one of timothy, that
in spite of the stone fences picked up from the

fields, the corn has to fight its way through the rocks, and that the push and prosperity of our great West are like unbelieved dreams to these hard-toiling mountain people. You saw the poetry of the daisies, the stone fences, and the picturesque huts. I am glad you did. I saw the reverse side."

"Yes, and when we climb old Marcy, you will be growling about the 'steep and brambled trail,' and just keep me discouraged all the way up," she pouted.

"No, I'll promise to sing 'Onward, Christian Soldiers,' all the way up, just as we used to in chapel."

"I wish Prexy were here to lead it for us."

"Thanks, awfully."

"Oh, not but that you *can* sing, Mr. Winake, but you won't half mean it."

They had gone into the parlor as they talked.

"Are you Mr. Winake?" said the bell-boy, coming from the hotel register. "Here is a telegram for you."

"Oh, already! It is my punishment, I suppose."

"I hope it is nothing—"

"It is from Holwell, saying he will be here tomorrow morning. Must have made the deal sooner than he expected."

"Then I shall have some sympathy."

"Yes, Holly is something of a dreamer."

"Well, he won't go to raising hay and corn the

first thing. He takes his hat off to nature."

" Not a descendant of William Tell, then."

" Do you think nature is a tyrant ? But I don't blame you if you can't discover her doing anything better."—

" Than raising corn ?"

" What shall we do with the rest of the day, Miss Berkeley?" It was after dinner. "I should like to take a walk if the condition of the natives won't distress you too much."

"Oh, no; I am a philanthropist by nature, and I may open a bureau of relief here."

" We can at least study the guide-book. Why, Marcy is not near here at all. It is beyond Keene Valley. We are not in the mountains at all yet. O yes, Hurricane can be seen in the distance. What would we do without our 'dear little blue book.' "

" I suggest a rest until Holly comes. He has been here before. What have we to read ?"

" I have just finished Howells' 'Quality of Mercy.' "

"A departure in psychology, isn't it ? "

" It is the best soul analysis we have in our new fiction."

"And yet, from a sociological standpoint, I do not like any of Howells' nearly so well as Garland's stories. Garland never seems afraid of conclusions. He states the definite wrong of society and attacks it manfully, often proposing remedies for distinct social ills."

"But is not the other truer art? Howells arouses all your indignation by his realistic conditions. You make your own conclusions, and propose your own remedies."

"It may be better art, but isn't art a little slow for the demands of the age? There isn't much art about the affairs at Homestead just now. I am convinced those poor men would like to do the right thing for their families and their fellows. Who shall tell them what it is? Their condemnation of the unfortunate anarchistic shooting is heroic, and confirms the public confidence in their integrity. Their hearts are right. What little art can do for them has been done. But who shall point them the way out?"

"Congress."

. "When was Congress converted?"

"In the campaign of '90."

"You know what I mean. When have the masses had a law from Congress as against the classes?"

"The McKinley——"

"Don't be foolish, Mr. Winake."

"Well, I wasn't going to say anything."

"You were in a fair way to say nothing. Nothing but the public conscience can open the way to toilers, nothing else can lead them out when it is open. The novelist of to-day finds here his greatest power. Just as the Teacher of Nazareth aroused by parables the conscience of his time, so now——"

" But did not Jesus' parables show consummate art in their concealment of ways and means ?"

" Certainly, for the time was not yet at hand. But after the enduement did Peter conceal anything? 'Ye have crucified him.' 'Repent.' To my mind that was the higher art, coming from the same spirit, for it brought immediate action. No one can deny the fullness of time this very minute in social reform. This is the golden day of letters. The editor, the moralist, the novelist, the economist, and even the preacher have come to their own at last. The pen is mightier than dynamite. The wielder of the pen alone can snatch the fuse from the anarchist's bomb. I would rather write the new 'Uncle Tom's Cabin,' than to do the honors of the White House."

" You think a woman will write it, do you ? "

"A woman wrote the first, why not ? "

" I admire the color in your cheeks and the almost terrible light in your eyes, Miss Leona. In fact, I feel myself yielding to your hypnotism, if not to your logic. But I must remind you that we are in the Adirondacks. Had you forgotten ?"

"I was dead, but am alive again. Let us go forth and worship."

" The churches are not open yet——"

" The churches ? " With a penetrating accent. "I spoke of the mountains."

"But don't you remember 'that neither in yonder mountain nor at Jerusalem ——"

"Your exegesis is musty, like your theology. The Jewish and Samaritan strife is supposed to have ended, or at least is transferred to new factions. After awhile we shall learn when and how to worship in Spirit. Churches then ·will be armories, not altars. Every spot will be an altar. All unrighteousness the foe."

Adrian's half-cynical mood died away as he walked beside this enthusiast for man and the home of man. A home made so beautiful, so sheltered and overflowing by the Creator, in mountain, in forest, and plain, but made so hard, and ugly, and empty for the millions, by thoughtless or designing men. The woman impulse began to take hold upon him with new and not unpleasant effect. He loved nature, he believed in the race, though he often groaned with anguish as he thought of the long journey and the meager progress of humanity. Unfortunately he had cultivated a light way of treating all serious subjects when with his friends, that gave one the false impression that he was both selfish and indifferent.

They walked, facing the setting sun, towards Deep Hollow. Just before them, like an emerald set in gold, was Cobble Hill in the last spreading light of the already hidden sun. Numerous hills lay on either hand, regular in outline, while to the south they grew larger and more broken. They were told that the road led to "Split-Rock Falls," eight miles to the southeast, a popular resting-day place for tourists stopping at Elizabethtown. Behind them Raven stood, proud, glossy black, in the soft sunset light. Returning they passed on down into the quiet village. They rested for awhile on the bridge, watching the eager little Bouquet scurrying away as though the night would catch it before it reached the lake. It did overtake it, and always will. It seemed to Leona as though the unfortunate were always hurrying just so, running from pain and poverty out to the realm of repose, but always overtaken by the night. It was still light enough to observe the sober colors of the water-worn rocks in the river. They were seal and clay, olive, bronze, and granite-green, drab and gray, ochre and white ; and yet when held up out of the water they looked very much alike. So it seemed to her, men, viewed under the light-refracting element of caste and vocation, appear much more dissimilar than upon close inspection. Under common emotions they act very much like the sons of a common father.

Is not each one a father, a son, or a brother? Will he not wince if you prick him? Will he not show gratitude if you caress him? If he suffer, will he not moan ; if he be happy, will he not laugh? If his own die, will he not weep? If he sin, will he not feel conscience's stinging reproof? If he die, will he not see visions this side the parting veil? If he live again, will it not be by virtue of his inheritance from the Eternal?

Wherein do men differ? Surely in nothing but judgment. Otherwise the same qualities obtain. The heathen mother strangles her baby girl; the Christian teaches hers chastity in the growing years. Each, because her Deity so commands her reason. Each obeys conscience and commits no sin—there is no guilt in either. But God pity the one if she teach not chastity!

No stern pen like mine can reproduce the fine, secret, womanhood emotions and purposes, sweeping through Leona Berkeley's gentle soul as she stood introspectively in the twilight, gazing on the bridge.

It was a communion hour without priest, wafer, or cup.

"Mr. Marveley, this is my sister Leona, and our friend, Mr. Winake. I know you will be friends in an hour. Mr. Marveley is an old classmate of mine at Andover. A quiet fellow then, he has made a great stir since. We all three read your new book, or rather Leona read it to us, on the boat last week. It is superb. I am proud of you."

"Very kind of you, I am sure. I happened to meet Holwell;" turning to Leona, " or 'Hollyhock,' as we used to know him at Andover, in New York. I was lounging towards the Catskills, but

you know his way, Miss Leona ; it is irresistible ;
so here I am."

"A regular four-in-hand."

" You will be pleased to learn, Leona, that Mr.
Marveey is fresh from the Homestead strike, intending to lay his next story there."

"That's a secret, Berkeley. We have to keep
the reporters off, or they will have the whole story
in the papers before I write a line."

" One woman, three men. Three to one we keep
it," said Winake.

"And no takers," quietly replied Leona.

" I am more pleased than I can tell you that you
can give us the very latest, and the facts, about
Homestead. I never wanted to go anywhere so
much in my life. And this will be almost as good.
I think I need not ask which side you take."

" There is but one side, to the thoughtful man on
the ground, Miss Berkeley."

" I was sure of it."

"Stage for Keene Valley," shouted the driver.

"We are ready," came back the hearty reply.
It was a glorious morning for a ride. Three other
guests were going along, making the wide, four-
seated mountain wagon a roomy, jostling, rattling
triumphal car.

" To the left you see the peak of Hurricane, pro-
nounced in three distinct syllables, with a world

11

of stormy meaning by the natives," shouted Holwell.

"Just in front of us is Saddle-back Hill. Can't you see the pigmy soldier seated on his steed, ready for the rush?"

"Not a soldier, Holly, let's call it the elfin rider. Make him the hero of your next story, Mr. Marveley."

"I beg your pardon," came from the back seat, "but is this Mr. Eugene Marveley?"

"It is," replied Berkeley, "and I shall be pleased to present you to him."

"We are a party of three from Boston," giving their names, "and have been in raptures over Mr. Marveley's stories, particularly the last one. We certainly regard the pleasure of meeting him as the chief thing of our visit."

"And just think of it, broke in one of the young ladies, to ride in the same wagon, and see the same mountains."

"I beg of you say no more," cried Mr. Marveley, as though the whole affair were a huge joke.

It is very easy for tourists to become acquainted. Often some long looked-for peak coming into sight suddenly, an accident of some kind, and sometimes only a smile is needed to make strangers confidential friends. A friendship this, foreign to the high-pressure life of every day. It results from a leveling environment. Exalted things make smaller ones more alike, and if they be men, cause them to draw closer together. When all men shall come to look up to the Highest they shall be brethren indeed.

For nearly seven miles they climbed up easy slopes, while the dashing Bouquet just at their side came down with many a mocking little laugh that anybody should want to go up hill. Often they listened to what seemed a shower of raindrops on the leaves up the hill, only to find shy, little falls of water with ten or twelve feet descent. After about an hour, every moment of which was filled with some swift-changing scene, they reached Pitch Off Pass, sheltered by a rugged cliff at a height of nearly two thousand feet. They have stolen upon Hurricane so stealthily that he stands for some moments in plain view, so near that it seems one could almost leap into his green depths, so illusive and alluring are mountain distances. A thousand feet below they sight the famed Keene Valley, stretching its ten miles of Italian beauty from Keene to the Au Sable ponds.

"How can I wait?" mused Leona.

"For what?"

"For the valley; it seems like heaven."

"I thought heaven was up, not down," said Adrian.

"Yes, some people do think they will find no heaven until they can fly. They don't know that it is a condition and not a place."

"Do you think they will ever discover their mistake?"

"I doubt it."

"Look! far beyond the ranges rising west of the valley, you can see White Face. You must look quickly however, or you will lose it. Next to Marcy it is the grandest pile in the Adirondacks."

As they descended rapidly, the Gothics, a distinct range within themselves, appeared to the south, while to the southwest a little later, Marcy itself was distinguishable."

"Isn't there an Indian name for Marcy?"

"Tahawus; a much stronger name every way. The fact that it is an Indian name makes it much more appropriate, even if it had no special significance; but meaning, as it does, 'I cleave the clouds,' it ought to be accepted without question."

"One reads," remarked Mr. Marveley, "that among the first summits to appear above the water in primeval times were these loftiest of the Adirondacks. Doubtless Tahawus was first to cleave the universal cloud, and White Face first to reflect the soft, prophetic light of life."

"Isn't it wonderful to think that here old mother earth began," half sighed Leona.

"I presume *terra firma* was uttered for the first time that day."

"How can you, Mr. Winake! Besides there were no days yet. Didn't the Dean teach you that the sun, moon, and stars were not made until in the third epoch, and that there was no distinction between the solar day and night until then ?"

"You forget I am not a theolog."

"Ah, yes," with a deeper sigh.

"Here we turn into the valley proper. Six miles further we will find St. Hubert's Inn (known for years as Beede's) and dinner."

In spite of the hot sun, the valley drive was cooled with a fragrant breath from off the hills which rise immediately out of the plains, in this respect unlike any other portion of the range.

"Every mountain range has an outline-figure peculiar to itself. Sometimes it is round, again sharp and peaked, but the Adirondacks take the long, wavy contour. Almost every conceivable shape can be seen along the horizon. A wealth of design worthy a sculptor. One could not easily tire of them for that reason," explained Mr. Marveley.

Passing Keene Valley post-office, they discover several beautiful cottages, maroon and yellow, nestled back on the first levels of the hills.

"What delightful nooks in which to hide from figures, pork and stocks," suggested Winake.

"While for the really tired, there is no rest," returned Leona.

Just after a long hill-pull they are at St. Hubert's, the most modern and inviting hotel in the Adirondacks. It is a whirl of civilization set down in the midst of majestic repose. Everything that eye or ear or palate is accustomed to in the outer world, or can wish, is here in profusion. What monumental stillness settles about it. To the east is Hopkin's Peak, and the Giant of the valley with its Sphinx-like I. V. W. in black and green. No mind has had the gift to read that dire secret of the ages. Some antediluvian giant may have carved his challenging initials as he strode from range to range in Homeric rage.

Between east and south is Noonmark, with its shadow-players appearing each day in a new role —"a pantomime of the angels," as a little friend of mine suggested. The east branch of the Au Sable River runs but a little distance away, drawing to its quieter level the falls of Roaring Brook, three hundred feet down the side of the Giant. Chapel Pond and the Giant's Washbowl are two other attractions in the Giant's great show, easily reached from the Inn.

"Now we shall rest," said Berkeley. "Early to-morrow we will start for the Au Sable ponds to find the chief of all the valley's charms. The Upper Au Sable for beauty, Tahawus for grandeur. And yet so many other lakes and mountains fall so little behind them, that discrimination is difficult."

"Now Mr. Marveley can tell us about Homestead."

"You will have a more sympathetic staging if we walk out a little way from the haunts of the guests," suggested Adrian. "Such an indiscreet gang of socialists as we, are liable to be mobbed by the aristocracy."

"The suggestion is a good one."

"Which half, Miss Berkeley?"

"Oh, you can't divide Mr. Winake's propositions. They have to be taken whole, like oysters."

"The supply of sauce seems to hold out well," replied Adrain sharply.

"Well, Russell's Falls are just a few steps away. We will go up there and save our necks," said Berkeley.

"Of course, you must understand," began the novelist, "that I did not go to Homestead in cold blood, for a story. That has been an after-thought, in fact, a necessity. I must overflow somehow. I will give it a channel. Perhaps my indignation and sympathy may do some good for other toilers, if not for the men at Homestead now.

"It was a strange experience. To see thousands of workingmen idle, even on a gala day, is a novel sight; but to see them dejected, solemn and smilelessly earnest, and waiting restlessly, is quite another sight. A whisky-laugh, now and then, just to bring out the soberness of the vast throng, a mocking, jeering face among five hundred, to deepen the lines of care and dread. To stand at one side and look upon such a crowd would quicken any pulse, but to become a man with them as I did, would almost stop the heart's beating. Some-

how they found out who I was. I think the post-
master gave them the information. You see, they
were watching for spies all the time. A number
of them had read 'A Toiler's Struggle,' and
trusted me from the first. They took me into their
homes and left me beside their sick babies. Never
accustomed to speak, I found myself addressing
vast throngs of men, quiet, orderly, but fearfully
grim. I refused again and again, until their reproachful eyes nerved me to the ordeal. I am not
sorry I did it. I was afraid of just what has happened. Rumors had already reached us, in fact,
open propositions from the anarchists, either to
remove the offending parties, or destroy the works.
A few only gave heed to the hiss of this serpent,
labor's most subtile and tempting devil. I rejoice
that every word of warning I uttered was ap-
plauded to the echo. I know the published pro-
tests of the strikers since the shooting to be truthful. They feel they have been most grossly mis-
represented and maligned by the bloody deed. I
thundered in their ears, by no trick of rhetoric, for
I know none, that anarchy seeks to bless by cursing, to heal with the dagger, and moves towards
its heaven through hell."

"What do you think of the issue, Mr. Marveley?"
asked Leona.

"It is difficult to say. One thing is settled forever, I take it. The Pinkerton bull-dogs will have
to stay in their kennels. Blood-hounds for slaves,

soldiers for freemen. One other thing has been settled. No private soldier will ever again be hung up by his thumbs, and branded with barbers' tools by the officer in command, on American soil. Perhaps a third fact is almost determined. A book entitled 'Triumphant Democracy' will have an increased sale.

"But, more generally; the people and honest labor asking its own, are closer by this strike; the day is nearer when the profits of money plus toil will be more equally distributed between capital and labor. The bitterest days are over."

"I am glad to hear you say that. I have been very apprehensive."

"No need of it, Berkeley. The anarchists will show their hand within three years. Few in number, mad in brain, and possessed in soul, they will be exterminated at a single blow. The separation between law-hating and law-abiding took place at Haymarket Square. A stream of blood is between them now. Its current was quickened at Homestead last week. It will never be crossed.

"The steadying hand of the teacher and the writer came just in time. Had no one called a halt and pointed another way, 'Cæsar's Column' would have been built ere this. The 'face about' has come. The army has been re-enforced ten-fold since then, from every profession and rank of life. The best, the wisest, the most relentless in battle, of America's sixty millions are faced now with labor towards its goal—just compensation. I include the noblest and most truly cultured women of the land."

"It is woman's problem more than man's," broke in Leona. "It concerns directly the home, its children, and its virtue. Sometime the anti and pro-tariff shouters will put their mouths in the dust and the protection of the home will stir every heart. The home-lovers for it; the home damners against it."

"Rostrum, rostrum," called Winake, who never could endure that a private conversation should become so serious and tragical.

"Miss Berkeley will doubtless take it when the conflict comes," musingly said Mr. Marveley, in Leona's defense, whose intelligent sympathy with current reform had strangely affected him. He was not accustomed to that sort of thing in the East. A bright, girlish, laughing young lady, evidently used to the best society, well-dressed, with an air of cultured repose when the occasion required, and yet so thoughtful, so well-read, so definitely set on one side or the other of every great question, was an anomaly to Marveley. What a character she would make, and, yes, what a friend she could be; and if a friend, what a helper.

Adrian saw the intense but unconscious expression on his face. Whether or not he himself had had any serious intentions toward Leona, he withdrew at once from the contest with a nobility native

to him, though not always on the surface. He
knew his advantage as a friend of the family, but
he saw the eternal fitness of things, and secretly
promised aid rather than interference.

Aroused from his revery by Leona's suddenly
uplifted face, as though to question him further,
Marveley went on : " I have not told you the chief
motive for going to Homestead. It is somewhat
painful, and yet not really so, after all. One of
the leaders of the strike is an older brother of
mine. So you see I am tied to that cause, and to
this particular issue, by a cord of flesh. He wrote
me for advice. I answered in person. Two of the
principal events of the strike were the result of his
high-minded and yet loyal fairness. I am not at
liberty to name them now. But you see, what I say
of the case I can vouch for. Above everything else
I have said or shall say, I want this to be heard :
Ninety-five out of every one hundred of these men
will protect any human life with their own. They
are not haters of men. I doubt if more can be said
of any ten thousand men in the world."

A peculiar feeling came over Adrian as he
learned how close Marveley was to the great conflict. First he felt a gulf sinking between them ;
in an instant he hated himself for it ; then a strange
longing broke through his whole being, spreading
like some fearful contagion. A longing to be one
of those helpless, hopeless men possessed him.
He arose from the rock-bench, and stepping out

into the open light, pretended to be looking away for some distant peak.

Truly he was looking away for that summit every soul of us feels compelled at times to climb toward. He walked a little way, until the placid music of the falls overcame the voices of the earnest talkers. The mood deepened upon him. He was almost alarmed. He struggled as a soldier might against the rising fever which he knows will keep him in camp and from the field. He was still looking out over the hilltops when he heard Leona's voice above the brook's waters for a moment. It came clear, searching, as a general's would in the midst of battle if it were a woman leading. Not an entranced Joan of Arc, but a brave, rational, race-loving woman. He felt impelled to look with more directness. All the good in him was rising and marshaling his forces. Self, the cynic self, the provoking, half-idle self, was laying down its flashing wit-sword, and his dead father's heroic spirit was taking possession, as by some new philosophy of post-natal transmigration of souls.

He looked again. Now he saw the summit. But a fearful consciousness had come with it. It was a frightful price he was paying for his redemption. *He loved Leona.* Loved her, not for her girlish beauty and winning ways, but for her womanly love of men, and her unyielding devotion to the cause of liberty. Loved her, and he had just pledged himself to aid another, a stranger, and one already in the full of her sympathy by their common interests, one whom the world called great. His pledge he would keep at all hazards. The summit he would reach, and alone.

By some strange impulse he felt moved to make immediate record of his awakening. Taking his diary, he wrote: "Russell's Falls, Adirondacks, July 26th, 1892, 4:40 P. M. Two revelations. One, the summit of my life: devotion to the cause of honest labor in America. The other begins and ends in myself. One complements the other; doubtless, one the cause, the other the effect. A. Winake." Poor fellow, he would analyze things by his old habit, though it killed him. However, the analysis helped him. He saw that the effect had come to take the place of the unattainable cause. Otherwise he would die. To have loved Leona Berkeley, and to have remained indifferent to the race, or lightly jesting to her impulses, would have been either to have lost her irrevocably, or having gained her, to chill her into a most wretched existence, bringing lifelong misery to both. She would at least respect him now—that he had the right to claim and to hold.

There was no great mystery in Adrian's sudden change. It was in his very nature. He had stifled these mercy-voices all his life. At college, where the environment was conducive to their development, he fought the harder against their influence.

But now a great desire had given him a great purpose. He had the true nature back of it.

I have talked with many an indifferent student to find a single sentence awakening ambition and purpose. Education means no less than this.

What surer teacher can there be than love?

I shall not undertake to account for what follows. Indeed, I am not sure that any explanation can be given. There are those who would say that this sudden uprising of Winake's nobility was the result of mind-influence—remote mind-influence. I am not a convert to that philosophy yet. There are strange things wholly believed by good men with strong minds. It is no longer a sign of weakness to believe in mental influence through space. But I am simply not convinced that it is not wholly subjective. I think the only mind influence in this case, however, came from Leona Berkeley's beautifully turned little skull, with its delicate quality of brain.

But you want the fact, and not theories, mine or theirs.

"A special delivery letter for you, sir," said the clerk to Winake, as they sauntered into the vast lobby of the hotel. Still tremulous with the emotion of his "revelation,". as he called it, it is not strange that he appeared very nervous as he tore the letter open.

" I hope it is only good news, Adrian."

Leona never had called him Adrian before. I
don't know why she did it now. Something in his
manner all the way from the Falls, a subdued,
gentle, sober mood, had impelled her to a sisterly
affection for him, particularly as he had appar-
ently been shut out of their councils. She had
already determined that the after-supper conversation should be literary, that Adrian might show
himself to better advantage before Mr. Marveley.

Pale as death, and with his lips a-quiver, he
handed her the letter and went out.

"Oh, dear!" she exclaimed as she read. "What
will the poor boy do?"

How it would have hurt him had he heard her, she
little knew. Her words meant that with his great
fortune gone what would become of him—poor
wretch. Yes, that was the total of it. A western
bank, in whose hands were all his large interests,
had failed. His attorneys wrote him that unless a
certain deal could be made, whose details neither
Adrian nor Leona had noted in the letter, the
thousand dollars which he now had with him in
drafts for his outing, would be the extent of his
wealth. Berkeley and Marveley read the letter.
Holly was fearfully distressed, even to tears. He
felt very much as Leona had expressed herself, but
with a man's greater knowledge of men's ways, he
knew that Winake could find something to do.

"Adrian would make a fine journalist. He has
just the tact to find, and the nerve to write up

news. That sarcastic cynicism of his would make spicy reading."

"Well, it just occurs to me," said Marveley, "that there is a first-class opening on the staff of the 'World,' where I have some influence, sufficient, I think, to secure a favor of this sort. You could recommend him Berkeley? It is a very responsible place."

"Indeed I can. I have always urged him to try reportorial work when he had finished at college. He has half-way promised to do it."

"I shall hope he will turn his sharp criticism for the cause of humanity. I ask no other return. The 'World' lies that way."

"I know him to be in full accord with current reform," said Leona, "though he likes to deny it. He is full of noble impulses. I thoroughly believe in him. But the shock will be so very severe."

"I presume he will have to leave us?"

"Oh, dear, I hope not," replied Leona.

"No, he must not," added Berkeley. "I think I can arrange it so that he will not feel it. If he can go to work early in September, there is no reason why he should not remain with us until that time."

"I will write at once to the 'World.'"

"Had we not better wait until we consult him? He may have some plans of his own," suggested Leona.

"I doubt it, but we shall wait. We are all very

grateful to you, Marveley, for this kindly aid.
Adrian is just like a brother to me. I must go
now and find him. I can do more for him than
anyone else."

He learned from the porter that Winake had
taken the path back to the Falls.

It was early twilight. Once or twice a late bird
sang a timid little trill far away. Adrian had
noted several flying across the open space in front
of the falls, hurriedly, as though hunted, and then
disappear in the sheltering woods. A pillar of
cloud rested on the broad summit not far away.
White at first, it caught soon the gold of the sunset. "A cloud by day and a pillar of fire by
night," thought Adrian. " I have crossed the sea.
That I know by the psalm that keeps chanting
itself within me. I have heard, too, the voice of
the leader. The promised land is far off, doubtless,
but in it is the heavenly mount."

He looked down at his feet. A massive, seamed
rock lay like the strength of ages beneath him.
Its up-reaching side was both a shelter and a
shadow ; under it was a gushing spring. At last
he had an image of the Absolute. David saw it
centuries before, but he had forgotten that. It
was his now.

" Well, my boy."

Berkeley had been afraid of frightening him
12

in his nervousness, and tried to approach in full
sight, but Adrian's in-looking had been too ab-
stracted. He looked up very calmly.

"It was kind of you to come, Holly. But I guess
I am all right."

"Of course you will be all right, Adrian. No
new thing has happened; new to you, but not to
the world. You have brains," he went on, not
wishing to give him time to despair but to have
hope at once, "and a splendid education. The
world has claims upon you. Now it stands a better chance of making them good. It looks like
providence, but at this very moment the way
opens for the fulfillment of your promise to me.
Marveley has at his command a vacancy on the
'World' staff. You can step at once into prominence as a young journalist. Your qualifications
are ample, and Marveley will prove a true friend
until you can gain some experience."

"They say losses make gains. I am sure mine
have. Such timely and courteous help is rare. I
thank you and Mr. Marveley and Leona for this
thoughtful kindness. But, Holly, I want to show
you something. I am glad I wrote it now. It will
prove that my determination is no spasmodic impulse, or nervous re-action. As you talked here
this afternoon, on this very spot, I had what I call
my 'revelation.' Of course that's the poetry of it.
In reality I came to myself; that is all. I have
been wanting to do so this long time, but didn't

have the courage, or motive, or, something. But read this and you will understand."

" This is exceedingly strange, Adrian. Its outlines are too large for me yet. I will grow to them by and by. I gather here that an hour before your sad letter came, you had resolved to go among the laboring men and with them strive for their ends."

" You are accurate in every word."

" The second revelation,—"

Adrian paled.

" I see that is all yours. I will not touch it. But may I ask a single question? You need not answer it unless you wish. I will tell you sometime why I ask. Had it any connection with the message you afterwards received—a mental forewarning of coming disaster?"

" I will answer. It had not the least."

Berkeley thought he had a gleam of light. But his face was blank. He would probe no further. It was a sacred secret, and should be respected.

He put his strong hand on Adrian's shoulder as they stood together. The significance of the great event was coming in on Berkeley. His fervent and poetic nature was aflame under the thought of it.

Here is work for an artist. A night-fall from the mountain tops, great shadows lying wide and deep upon the valley, cut by a thin wedge of light entering through a distant pass, touching with silver the water against the rocks, showing against the side-shadows the faces of two men. It is a

Pauline fellowship: "Fraternity vaunteth not itself, is not puffed up, thinketh no evil, rejoiceth in all things." The little valley is a baptismal font; the fading light the sacred element; the Holy Spirit is breathed upon them from the stillness overhead.

There were no words from either. Words were in the moving trees, in the early stars, in the fastness of the great Tahawus, in the waving air. Everywhere the universe was vocal. It had the sound and the spirit of the Beatitudes.

"You would rather not see anyone, Adrian, until morning?" ventured Holly.

"It would be better."

"In the meantime Leona and Mr. Marveley shall know all, and our meeting in the morning will be as usual. Good night, and don't stay here long. I haven't a single fear for you, though. For it was from a mountain that the Brother of men went down to the furious sea and its frightened prey in the fishers' boat. Calm begets calm. So vast was His repose after the mountain-prayer, that nothing could roar or surge or wreck in His presence. So much greater was His repose after the sepulcher, that even the riot of sin grew still before Him. Keep to the repose you have found, and you shall be a soother of men. Good-night."

"Good-night."

Calm, and yet astir with emotion such as he had never known even in dreams before, we leave him

with the night, so like him in its repose, yet the
energies of life are beating doubly quick under its
shadows.

"This is the Adirondack Mountain Reserve,"
explained Berkeley, as they drove through a wide
gate early the next morning, paying a toll of one
dollar for the privilege. "It is a private park of
twenty-two thousand acres in the possession of an
incorporated syndicate. They have made an ex-
cellent drive-way through it to the lower Au Sable
pond, three miles and a half. They have cut several trails to the top of the mountains; and besides building the boat-house we shall soon see,
they have stocked the lakes and streams with fish,
intending to preserve one spot untouched by commercial hands."

Many charming views were had as they rolled
smoothly along over the solid road. The woods on
the right hand presented a peculiar appearance.
The foliage of long, slender maples and poplars
was not so dense as that of the pines, but gave the
sun its share of the space. As a result, designs
innumerable of quivering shade and sun-color were
all about the slopes. It seemed like some primeval palace alight for the return of its regal occu-
pants. A "chasm," of which Berkeley had forgotten the name, attracted them from their seats
to gaze into its quiet depths of water. "Stairway

Falls" they christened a broad expanse of rock cut away in steps down a slight decline, with a narrow strip of flowing carpet lying its length. Leona was much impressed with several huge rocks by the wayside, upon whose bare surface trees stood. They did not get their life from the rock, but through large roots which ran across and down on all sides of the stone into the ground.

"Of what do they remind you, Mr. Marveley?" she asked.

"Of the struggle for life the thousands have to make. Their barren homes do not seem to give them sustenance at all, but over the rock of their poverty you will find the roots piercing the mould of love and fellowship; not always of high order, to be sure, but it is better than nothing."

One of these was so odd they halted to examine it. A large tree growing at the edge of the rock had broken and fallen across it. A branch which pointed down its side had imbedded itself in the earth and become a root, while another standing out from the upper surface of the log, had grown straight up into a slender but symmetrical tree.

"That," cried Leona, "is an illustration of the desperate makeshifts that the many have to make. For religion, for hope, for content, the natural roots of every normal life, they are compelled to distort love of sick children, a single year's steady employment ahead, and satisfied stomachs once a week. And yet out of it all will sometimes grow a slender but beautiful life, like that young girl we saw in the city last week, secretary of the Associated Charities, grown from a ragged tenement-rat to an educated, refined, Christian young woman, helping others. But oh, how rare!"

"There is the lower Au Sable at the foot of the hill, with the boat-house to the left," shouted Holly.

"And that must be Indian Head further on to the left, looking up the lake," were the first words Adrian had said since they set out, beyond the usual morning greetings. They had respect for his silence and had made no attempt to break it.

"How stern he looks," he continued, "from the profile view, as though angry over his brutal loneliness. The sole remnant of a race whose only history lies almost obliterated in these mountains."

"Yes," said Marveley, catching the fine mood of his awakening compatriot, "below him are his three watch dogs set one just above the other on the rising levels of the hills. In the rough, but a noble design for a master-piece representing the irony of fate—the chief and his dogs waiting the coming of justice to his people. The very vultures above his head scream, 'Too late! too late!'"

"Beyond on the same side is Mount Colvin, rising two thousand feet sheer from the lakes. But on the right is my favorite in the Keene Valley, Mount Ressagonia, lying the full length of the ponds. See how it is terraced, tier after tier of regular buttresses. Now as we row opposite its broad side, look straight at its wealth of wood and tell me what you see," commanded Holly.

"Thousands of slender, straight, creamy-white columns, supported by a canopy of green."

"Yes, the finest growth of birch I have ever seen. Try the echoes, Leona, I want to note the difference in quality between yours and a man's voice."

She uttered a sort of swelling, crooning strain, which came back with the same volume and timbre, a second Leona.

"I wish I could find the hidden Leona in Ressagonia," sighed Adrian to himself; "I would not pledge her away before I knew whether I loved her or not."

"The guide has something for us, I think. He is pulling into the left shore."

"Take a little rest up here, if you wish. The famous 'ice cave.'" They sprang ashore. "I presume," calmly said Marveley, "these huge rock crevices are filled with ice in the winter, giving it its queer name."

Holly smiled as he watched them climbing the easy ascent.

"Why, how cool it is," shouted Leona, as Adrian gently handed her up to the mouth of the deep cave.

"Freezing," cried Marveley.

"Look down, and you will understand," exhorted Holly.

"Oh, I see piles of snow and ice," shivered Leona.

"Yes, for generations, probably ; perpetual ice."

From balmy, restful, echoing Au Sable to frigid ice caves, and at a single step.

"Extremes in life often lie closer than these," said Adrian, scarcely conscious he was being so personal or so revealing. It was said without bitterness, and I think chiefly with an eye upon the condition of the society he was so soon to enter. A new quality had come into his voice, a new manner; a sort of clinging in his bearing towards Leona. He did not know it. It was a part of the new relationship he had determined upon for them in his coming work. She clung to his hand as he helped her down the rocks, and into the boat, so friendly, as though begging for his confidence, that he almost forgot everything else but his resistless yearning to tell her all his plans and purposes. It was later than two o'clock the night before when he sought his room. Holly knew he would not leave the night until he had definitely fixed the future in his own mind. Adrian wondered if he could tell her part and not all. Better nothing than to violate his pledge.

A walk of a mile along the silver thread which connects the two ponds brought them to the upper Au Sable. Its two miles of water reflect some famous piles : Boreas, Haystack, Basin, Saddleback, the Gothics and Ressagonia. Here nature seems to have rested for an age, leaving her tenderest smile and most artistic touch upon the broken surface of the earth.

But the emotions of my hero are too strong to keep him in longer silence, even on silent Au Sable. The light lunch is ended. Marveley and Berkeley are smoking, Adrian and Leona have gone by common impulse to a huge rock overhanging the pond. As they lean over its edge they can see their forms reflected clearly in the deep mirror.

" What a shadowy picture of ourselves. Which, after all, is real, the shadow or the substance? Perhaps we saw our souls then, Leona ? "

She looked at him in ill-concealed astonishment. This was not his usual style of opening a conversation. Generally it was by jest, or some keenly critical remark concerning one's self, or situation.

" I hope our souls are not out of us to stay."

" I feel as though mine had just entered after a frightfully long absence. I had really doubted sometimes whether I had any. I think my closing work in the University, a birds-eye view of all philosophies, showing a general convergence towards the Absolute and Immaterial, and then a close and crutinizing study of the nature of Life and its relation to the Infinite, did more than all the sermons I ever heard to make me understand that if there is no soul and no Absolute, there is not anything; then our very senses deceive us; we are only a bundle of nerves; when the band breaks we fall apart and are not. But I shall worry no more about that. I am convinced so thoroughly now, that I know a single human life is worth more than the whole world."

"And this is my old friend Adrian talking to me?" tenderly smiled Leona up to his face.

"Never so much your friend as now."

"And never so respected and cherished as now," she responded.

Already he had found what he had set out to win through years. Perhaps—but no, a broken pledge would be a poor beginning. Then it was too late anyway. Doubtless this very happiness of hers, so open and brotherly, was an overflow from some deep emotion Marveley had set in motion by his love.

" I thank you for that, Leona. There is a world of help in it for me. May I lay one of my plans before you?"

"Nothing would please me so much."

" You know I have to enter the lists unarmed now. I had intended to take all my fortune and expend it in education of, and in homes for, the poor. But that dream is past. I go now simply a working-man with the rest. But I have a plan. I shall widen the circle as there is need."

For more than an hour he talked earnestly, seriously, almost dramatically at times, so much unlike himself, that Leona could only wonder as she listened.

"You see, its central fact is a regard for all human life. A hopeful appreciation of what life is, and can become. A sort of practical working of the Declaration of Independence, isn't it? 'Life, liberty, and the pursuit of happiness.' It is evolutionary in its tendencies, rather than revolutionary, and yet it need not be so very slow in bringing forth results. It would have been different a hundred years ago. The age is ripe for it now. Do you think it visionary?"

"I never heard of anything more practical, or abounding in common sense."

"Then I am satisfied. But, Leona, my great lack will be in myself. My plan will succeed in time. Working-men will trust me. But there will be days when I shall be weary and ready to die with the suspense, with the scorn and hatred of the men whom we must oppose. Many of them are my own friends, who never will comprehend the work. My soul cries out for some steady hand, some cheery heart, some strong companion."

He scarcely knew what he said. He was like one caught talking to himself, when he realized what his words meant. Something in Leona's face alarmed him. He sprang to her; but she smiled before he reached her, saying: "It's nothing. I

think looking at the water has made me dizzy.
Let us go down now."

What did it all mean? Not for the world would
he have said what he had, believing that it could
give her pain, and hurt both their lives. What
could he have been thinking about! It made him
almost rudely cold as he walked back to the
luncheon ground. Leona busied herself mechanically, as Adrian could see, putting away the dishes
and preparing for their return.

It was rather a silent little group on the home-
ward way. Marveley was thinking of another secret which he had not let even these dear friends
into yet. Berkeley was watching Adrian in the
seat in front of him, wondering what he would do
in his place, and smiling to himself, half-amused,
half-contented, as he thought of the "second revelation." Adrian was silent between two moods. One
of self-reproach for his ill-timed words. The other
of hope for his plan. It was not all his own. A
little coterie of them at the University had often
talked it over; it was their joint property. It had
been only an ideal. None of them ever dreamed
of advocating it seriously. It grew out of a debate
on political parties. It looked to the gradual
effacement of every issue but that of ill-paid labor
and its consequent conditions. It was just such a
plan, sprung from college enthusiasm and stand-
ards, as Gladstone would have wrought out had
he been an American instead of an English states-

man. Adrian was wondering now if he could get any of the seven others in the original band to share the issue with him. He must have some co-workers soon, for the plan meant a personal visiting of every one hundred workmen in the country. He had that morning counted over his private resources and discovered that nearly five thousand dollars was still intact. No one had lost but himself; he was under no obligation to restore anything to any man. With that sum he could get his work well under way, he thought. Help would come. He had decided to ask Leona to get Mr. Marveley interested in the plan, when his eager words at the Pond had prevented. If only he would enter with him, he could more easily endure his own great loss.

Leona thought—well, she has kept them close, very close, for a woman; I cannot record them.

They were very tired. The soft beds and cool rooms of the Inn seemed like a paradise of rest. What realities were fashioned in dreams before the sun rose, I cannot say.

They were all aglow with the morning's glory, when the porter shouted, " Stage for Lake Placid."

Down the valley, then to the west, and on to the beautiful lakes, they were carried. They crossed the third range of mountains west of Lake Champlain, slowly climbing up, until at an elevation of two thousand feet they suddenly emerged in full view of Cascade lakes lying between Long Pond

Mountain on the north and Pitch Off on the south. A perfect wilderness of crowding hills close one in at this point, until the feeling of smallness and utter dependence comes to even the bravest. The lakes are long and very narrow, with only a rivulet between. On the right is the Cascade House, a stroke of red and yellow against the green and gray. Opposite it, a cascade falls nearly six hundred feet from the edge of the wall-like mountain, to the lake, like a measuring-line.

After a prolonged rest and relished refreshment, they push on and out upon the broad plain of North Elba, coming soon within the horizon which makes Lake Placid so famous. For the first time Mt. Tahawus comes into splendid view. The Gothics lie this side of Tahawus with their many queer outlines, the 'Elephant's Back' clearly discerned. Then Colden, remarkable for its abysses, and great McIntyre, between which and Wall Face the Indian Pass links the west with the east. What a trail of aboriginal commerce it was once! What a desolation now!

Leaving these to the left and rear, John Brown's old farm comes into sight along the Au Sable river, on an inviting hill summit, where, beneath a monumental boulder, his body, but not his marching soul, lies.

Then the great hotels of Lake Placid came into sight; by-and-by an unsightly little village, just before reaching the loveliness, serenity, and peace of Mirror and Placid lakes, restful at the foot of old White Face, most beautiful and most loved of all the Adirondacks. White Face is the only mountain that smiles. Its broad expanse of countenance seems to greet you with good cheer and a royal welcome which at once puts you in a good humor and gives a comfortable home feeling.

"And that is White Face; dear old grandfather. I love him already," Leona chirruped.

"No matter how often you go away, or how long you stay, he will always be here smiling when you come back," said Holly. "Now for the first time I really feel at home. A good supper, a ride on Sweet Mirror lake, small, but so entrancing, so wooing, and then sleep beneath White Face's watchful eyes! Oh, this is life, happiness, wealth, everything!"

Even Adrian had quit eyeing Leona with half scared little glances in an attempt to read her thoughts, and had turned to the wonderland about them. Away to the south the great barricade of mountain peaks stands insurmountable. One forgets first the world, then himself, but comes back with God by and by, to self and to the world, a new creature.

"I must have my mail the very first thing," shouted Marveley, going on ahead of the others into the hotel. As they entered later, they saw him intently reading a tinted and scented little square paper, with a singular but silent smile. He

looked up as they came in, and put it away carefully in his inner pocket with a little pat, as much
as to say, "Quiet my heart a little in there, if you
can."

The hour was late. They were about to break
the little group into its constituent atoms for rest.
The converse had been high and strong. First, of
books, in which Adrian had shown himself a master far beyond Marveley's guesses, and often beyond his range, for he had been a student of men
rather than of books. Then they talked of the
problems of the hour. Leona had drawn Adrian
out, until, diffused with warm blood, his face had
shone as in a transfiguration, as little by little he
unfolded his plan. It was marvelous how it took
hold of them—a new demonstration of his power
over men. Marveley came over, and extending his
hand, said, "I want to be just behind the origina-
tor of that inspired scheme for the uplift of labor.
Everything I have, and can do, belongs to it from
this hour."

Adrian's eyes were full of tears of glad surprise.
He could not say a word. Berkeley promised immediate aid. Leona alone sat apart, silent. What
had happened? Had he been too bold? Had he
told them secrets she wanted kept for herself
alone? No, she was not a selfish woman. But
something was wrong. There was a half terrified
look upon her face. Then it came to him. Mod-

13

estly he thought of it; with a great swell of joy at
first; and then a quiver of dread. She doubtless
had promised either Holly or Marveley to receive
the latter's suit with favor. She was discovering
now too late that it was a mistake; that her life
and work ought to be with Adrian.

Just then Marveley sat down again. "As this is
a night of confidences, I have one." Taking the little fragrant missive from his pocket, he said, " I
beg leave to read a line from this. It is from a
beautiful young woman in Boston, whom you will
all love some day, I know. She is an artist, but
loves the race, and, the strangest part of it all, she
loves—me. And in answer to a question I asked
her recently, having begged time for a decision,
she writes very sweetly and modestly, as follows :

"*Dear Eugene:* After several days of quiet and
calm looking within and without, especially upon
your face upon my easel, I find it the happiest moment of my life when I write—will it make you
very happy, my dear—that little word, the mountain peak of the English language—' Yes.'

" HELENE."

Oh, joy ! oh, rapture ! Life's aglow. There's
warmth and hope everywhere. Oh, to-morrow.
All things are good, yea and forever!

They are leaving the room after congratulations,
and a second good-night. Adrian still standing at

the piano, called very softly : "Leona, can you stay
a moment ? "

"Yes, Adrian, if you want me."

"I do."

A CHRISTMAS STORY.

THERE were voices everywhere. The music of the crystals underfoot seemed like clear, tinkling bells to the merry throngs crossing, turning and parting at every corner of the streets. Under the glare of the street lamps just lighted, the convolutions of the great crowds at these center points of turning seemed like some splendid spectacular phenomenon of the stage.

But to a little, old man who, with hanging head and knotted brows, impatiently halted until a group of heedless children should get out of his way, there was rhythm neither in the graceful throng, nor in the crystals. The latter was like the sharp, shrill shrieking of discontent and restlessness; a hissing, jeering insinuation, reminding him of the sneers of one who darts a suspicious glance into your face, hoping to take you unawares.

But the crystals were not to blame, for the children's voices were not more musical to him. They were lisping a single refrain. Their eyes, their dancing feet, and gracefully gesturing arms, as well as their birdling voices, were all singing. They were extemporizing from that old theme, the

(196)

ground of all the music of childhood, whether of voice, or motion, or desire : "To-morrow, oh, how delightful !" But to him it was even more discordant than the song of the frost; he could grind under his feet the noisy ice-singers. The other song seemed like that strange key-note every structure, great or small, is said to have, which if prolonged under proper conditions will set the whole mass vibrating, slightly at first, until afterwards it sways beyond the law of its equilibrium and falls. It is not sympathy between the mass and the vibrating string, but a law of its nature.

To this nervous old man it was exceedingly distressful; and every new group of merry little ones he encountered shook him deeper, until in wretched unrest he reached his own door. He would not admit that he was irresolute, or less determined now than in the morning of this "day before Christmas." "It was all nonsense, and the relic of a superstitious barbarism; the remnant of a faith which civilization was having some difficulty to remove from the human mind, so desperately do these fools cling to their savage ancestry." A philosopher ? Why not ? Discontent has made the greater part of the philosophy of every age.

Into a not uncomfortable house did the heavy door open in obedience to his nervous pushing; the appointments were maintained with a considerable degree of taste. But while the flameless fire in the great Westminster did all it could under the dignity of a scientific process of burning to brighten up the rooms into which the shadow of the night was fast creeping, it had little success.

The easy elegance which half slept under the steady glow of the anthracite fire did nothing to calm the irritation which had unaccountably possessed him. On the contrary, it made him remember, in spite of himself, the open fire on the hearth, of his distant boyhood—distant by far more than intervening years; distant by changed thoughts and broken ideals, and immeasurably distant by reason of a buried faith, from whose sepulchre rock the seal had not been broken since the betrayal, trial and crucifixion of that spirit of trust given him in the very pain-throes of birth, inspired by every. look of his beautiful young mother, whose only life had been her boy and her unyielding trust. I will not relate how a Judas-like love of money brought about this death within him.

When by his command the gas was lighted, and the luxurious comfort of the room aroused itself and did its best to welcome and cheer him, all a-glitter with life, he still felt no better. The flash of the gas-light from the many jets only brought to mind the flickering candle-light of those other distant days. He saw the tall, yellow " dip." with the miniature lake of fuel at its summit, which was constantly pumped into the flame to feed its quiet burning, by the currents which played about the slowly-consumed wick—the puzzle of his boyhood. Its rich, yellow light, not dazzling but mild, bathed table and ancient books, spinning-wheel and sanded floor in a wave of soft illumination, until now, as he recalled it, with the face of his mother in the midst of it, it seemed like the picture of some German master, the sweet-faced woman its glory, about whom the candle-light played, a halo of blessed hallowing.

Then there was the first Christmas of his recollection. They had placed the candle on the table but had not yet lighted it. They were content, she and he, in the milder baptism of the wood-flame. His head had lain upon her knee, as he sat on the low stool at her side, feeling the pressure of her warm clinging arm around him. He had gazed into the slowly dying flames with that fixed stare which so irresistibly possesses one before an open fire, while his quick imagination peopled the hearth with the heroes and heroines of the delightful old-fashioned story she was telling him.

After a long silence, he had, without taking his eyes from the fire, or moving his head from its resting place, softly asked her to tell him once more the story of the baby Christ. As her voice grew low and gentle, but trembling with the pathos of her great mother-heart, as she thought of Mary in the Judean inn, so needy, in so trying an hour, he pictured it all in the coals and pieces

of charred wood.   Yonder in the far corner of the
fire-place, where the shadows lay deep, he fancied
the shepherds were silently watching; a number
of burnt-out coals, white with their ashes, were
the sleeping sheep.   Suddenly a "chunk" falling
from its place, against the iron, sent up a bright
flame for a moment, that shone far into the dark
corner, and started the shepherds to their feet.   In
the blue tips of the flame he could see the dim
outlines of angels' faces, while the lengthening,
waving and turning flames seemed to make long
folds like the robes he had always imagined the
angels wore.   It needed but the rising wind without, to make the music for them, and angels and
chorus of song were all there.

Then he had turned his eyes to the other corner
of the hearth where it was still darker.   There, he
thought, stood the inn where the babe was born.
Three huge coals, lying out alone from the fallen
"chunk," were the three wise men seeking the
new-born King.   He had only to shut his eyes
tight to see the wondrous star hanging over the
dark corner, and the three bright coals moving
closer and closer.   He had lain there a long time
with his eyes shut, when the dark corner grew
strangely bright and beautiful; he saw the babe
in its mother's arms, like the picture in the big
Bible, and the wise men with their arms full of the
most lovely presents.   He thought the mother
looked so happy, and the child so wise, as if he

knew all that was said and done, when suddenly
he heard his own mother's voice close down at his
ear, calling his name gently. He had fallen asleep
while she talked. He shivered as he awoke, for
the room had grown cold.

And now under the gas-light and fire-glow of his
splendid home, the old shivering came back upon
him, just as the other memories had come, only
the strange trembling was more real. He tried to
steady himself against the great chair in which he
sat, but a hot flush in his face, and his trembling
hands, told him something was wrong.

"Must have worked too hard at the books to-
day," he muttered. "That confounded bookkeeper has got 'em into a muddle that is enough
to give anybody a nervous chill." He managed to
get to his own room, and ringing for his servant,
gave directions for his relief.

As he had entered the door earlier in the evening, a fluttering dress might have been seen at the
head of the stairs. And let me tell you before
you guess it, that it belonged to as beautiful a
child as ever called a cross old man "grandpa."
Her face glowed like a bunch of roses whenever
she could win a caress from him, for somehow she
loved him in spite of his crustiness. He always
seemed to be troubled about something, and she
never blamed him for anything he did. Such faith
do children have in us in spite of ourselves. For
a half hour she had been peeping from the turn in

the winding stairway, to see " if grandpa had any
bundles when he came in." Something in the way
the door was pushed open told her he had none,
and she just succeeded in getting out of sight as
he entered.

" Well," she declared, " if he had just brought
one tiny little bundle I would have forgiven him
all he said about Cousin Ben and Christmas, this
morning; but *now*, well—oh, I suppose I will have
to give it to him, but I don't believe he will ever
look at it, or at me either. But then I know he is
feeling bad about something, for Uncle Jo said
something was going wrong in grandpa's accounts
down town. Oh, dear, I hope his bookkeeper won't
catch the absconda—something, I've forgotten now
what it is, and have to be sent away to Canada,
like the one at Jennie May's papa's bank. That
was just awful; and what if grandpa should get it
too, oh, dear!" beginning to relent already.

Just then her mamma called her—for she and
her mamma and brother Gilbert lived with her
grandpa, to "make home for him," as she expressed it. She called her to come down stairs,
for grandpa was not feeling very well, and had
asked for her.

"Asked for me?" and her bright eyes danced,
while she almost forgot his sickness in the joy of
being "asked for." She started to throw a strand
of gold beads about her neck, but remembering
that they were his only Christmas present to her,

she was afraid he might take it as a hint for another. She rushed away without them to the room her grandpa called his own, and was ready to say something cheerful to him as she pushed the door open gently, to "take him by surprise;" but when she saw his pale face, as he sat propped up in bed, he looked so tired and worn, and full of pain, that she caught her breath, and tip-toeing towards him, almost sobbed, as hard as she tried not to.

He opened his eyes feebly, as she came up to his side, and putting out his hand drew her to him. Never could she remember such a mark of affection from him. It touched her so that, half frightened as she was, she hid her face in the great white pillow beside his, yellow and wrinkled with a lifetime of hard thinking, and sobbed piteously.

He spoke to her gently, saying he was not very ill; that he would be up and around to-morrow; that it was Christmas eve, and he guessed, if the porter at the office didn't forget it, there would be a box brought up before morning; he didn't know just what all was in it, but he guessed it was something good little girls with blue eyes would like, if a certain good little girl didn't rub her eyes too hard.

"Oh, grandpa, I am so sorry—but I can't tell you about it; I thought maybe you wouldn't—you hadn't; no, I did not think anything of the kind.

Something else thought it, I didn't, so there. I knew all the time you were the best grandpa in the whole world."

A sudden paroxysm of pain forced a moan from him as she finished speaking. A pain in both his hearts, but that in the inner heart was the keener of the two, and lasted much longer. She was too alarmed to speak, but he patted her hand, as much as to say, "It will be over in a moment." To her question, if she should call her mamma, he shook his head. After a moment he inclined his head toward her on the pillow, and half whispered: "Tell me about Christmas, Enie; do you love it?"

"Love it, grandpa? Indeed I do."

"Why?" he asked quickly.

She was more than alarmed at his queer look, but being a brave little body, she tried to answer him. She was about to say, "Because I find out how much everybody loves me then," when it seemed to her that would be out of place now. She thought of the Christ story she had so often read, and dreamed about, but somehow she had always been afraid to speak to him about Christ. She stopped a moment, as if to analyze her new feeling, for it seemed just right to speak to him to-night. After looking closely at his face, for the light was turned low, to see if his eyes were open, and finding them closed, she rested her head against his hand, as if to think the better, and began:

"Oh, so many years ago, long before your grandpa was born, I guess, a little child was born across the ocean. Some shepherds heard about it, from a band of singing angels, and were so glad that they began to sing, and ran to find Him, for it seems they had been expecting Him for a great many years, although I don't exactly understand how they could know. And they were so glad, that when Christmas comes, for He was born on Christmas, you see, I always feel glad too. There is a song in one of my books about it, and I always sing it now on Christmas morning."

"Won't you sing it now?" he asked.

She sang for him in that sweet, pleading voice of childhood the first verse of "On Judean Hills Afar."

Had the light been brighter she could have seen the tears running down his cheeks, but she went on: "They brought Him presents, because He was a present to them from God. I can't quite understand why God should have taken Him away from them so soon, but mamma says it was to make them love Him more; that they were cruel to Him while He lived, but that after He died they began to love Him still better."

"Yes, they loved Him when it was too late to do Him any good," muttered the old man to himself.

"But the Bible says it did *them* good, after all, to love Him, for His Father has a great house with thousands · of rooms, one for everybody who comes to live there."

" Yes, room enough for those who love Him; yes, we ought to love Him—He is merciful," speaking to himself in a feeble tone.

"And that is the reason why I love Christmas, don't you, grandpa? Don't you, grandpa?" she repeated.

"I guess he is asleep. I'll call mamma;" and she stole out of the room, not knowing she had been a gracious present to him on that strange Christmas eve.

He had known the Nazarene Christ in his early years, when his mother still lived; let us hope his head rested again upon her bosom, her arms about him, and that the fire-fancies glowed and brightened into the great Christ-Land, as a child, long wandering and long forgetful, returns to the old homestead to die. God is merciful, and childhood winning.

ODUNA.

Where the majestic Mississippi bends with a great, sweeping curve towards the Illinois forests, just below the little village of Okoth, some miles south of Quincy, is a little old colony of "New Yorkers." Fifty or sixty years ago they came to this river-bend, and took it by the might of a squatter's sovereignty. Some of those who were children then have grandchildren now, and feel a sort of kinship with the old river whose mid-channel currents, heedless and strong as death, have stopped not in all the years, whether marked by birth, marriage or unwakeful sleep.

It is a magnificent view which stretches out before a little group, on the morning of which this tale relates. The great, matchless river goes hurrying by, far out in its age-worn channel, sending into the shore, as its only recognition of other life than its own, little ripples of faint laughter that waste into sighing on the pebbled beach. To the innocent children these wavelets smile, winning and friendly, as they yield their soft, plump, little feet to their embraces; but to the two or three old men still living from the original settlement, it seems like the mesmeric smile of a demon, the Mephistopheles of the great valley.

They never forget his fierce, revengeful moods, when the long, dashing rains lash and prick him into fury, arousing his winter-cooled ire, until he hurls himself down his path, boiling and roaring, heaving, in angry breathings, his contortioned body further and further inland, seeking for victims with whom to appease his wrath. His rage seldom subsides until his passion has been glutted.

On this day the oldest of the ancient men sits in a deep reverie. His head is bowed upon both his hands, clasped over his old hickory staff; he hears not even the prattle of the children at his feet. Indeed, his favorite, a little girl, with eyes so strange and yet so winning that one at first starts back, and then comes at once to touch her, fails to catch his glance, though she tries more than once to have him look upon her.

He lifts his face at last, but a film of tears hides all but the river; it seems, through his sorrowful veil, to stretch itself into some slimy, threatening monster, from whom he would fly, but cannot. His thoughts are running back through the years, more swiftly than a bird flies back to its nest before the storm. He had again noticed, as they sat upon the rock that morning, a peculiar look in the face of the girl. It came to him for the first

time just the day before. He wondered now that
he had not seen it long ago.

She was his great-grandchild; her father had
been the eldest son of his only daughter, and he
was just discovering that she was taking on the
form and actions, indeed, the very features of the
woman who was once his babe, his tender girl, and
at the last the very affection of his heart. The
child's face, and a long scar on his own cheek, of
which a few moments before he had caught a feeble reflection in a shell filled with water, which
she had held up to his lips, laughingly begging
him to drink, had borne him back as waves bear a
disabled ship back to the dangerous shore, from
whence it sailed. It seemed to him that he had
returned and was fighting with the perils he
remembers now better than the events of yesterday.

When Oduna, his daughter,—the child bore the
same name—was sixteen, she met, on a great fete
day, a young soldier, a proud, overbearing,
haughty, handsome boy of twenty-one. She loved
him, gentle as she was, because he was so daring,
so defiant; but she loved him chiefly because he
could be so tender to her. His proud form bent
gracefully to caress, and hot words died away into
gentlest whispers when she came near him, such a
spell does love hold over its own. She was a
beautiful girl, not queenly, nor stately, but beau-

14

tiful with the grace of winning ways and a lovely
face. . She stood always, innocently, with a poise
of dependence and helplessness that made her admirers her defenders at once.   Her blue eyes were
like deep, living crystals, warm and wooing.

Her father saw only.the scornful, lofty bearing
of the young soldier; thus do men conceal themselves from each other.   In his uniform he unques-
tionably looked a fearless, and one might guess, a
reckless youth.   Such a contrast was there between
him and the gentle Oduna, that the father trembled for her happiness when he saw how fond of
him she was becoming.   He sought with a few
wise words to turn her heart from him before it
should be too late.   But it was too late even as he
spoke; she had pledged herself to her lover, and
she was as firm as she was affectionate, in spite of
her mild manner.   She told her father confidently
all she hoped from, and believed of her hero, until
at last he gave reluctantly his consent—not consent, for that he never gave—but he offered no
denial when together they asked his favor.   Most
lovingly did he bless them after the long service
at the old church-altar was finished.

They began their journey at once to the West in
company with a number of friends and relatives.
They took up their way, sad to leave so much behind, but glad with a great hope for the future.
Into the trustful heart of Oduna came the best and
most precious hopes, looking to the new home

somewhere in the great valley toward which they
were slowing moving. Her soldier husband had
given up his army life with all his ambitions to
become a leader of men, and gave a willing hand,
with much good cheer, to the preparation for the
journey; long on the way, he was guide and
scout for the whole party, fearful of no foe, and
dauntless.

The elements of our poor human nature are
strangely blended. So strong in danger, so ready
in battle, after the first few weeks of the monot-
onous journey wore away, when to be the guide of
a peaceable company of emigrants no longer
seemed so great a lot, and missing the comrade-
ship and cheer of the camp, the impetuous youth
became less companionable, and more silent and
moody, almost to sullenness. There was no change
in his treatment of Oduna. I doubt if there ever
should have been. But to all others he seemed
impatient, discontented, and given to taking his
own course in a masterful way. Often did they
yield to him in the face of their better judgment,
fearful to awaken something that lay hidden within
him, half slumbering but alive.

Whether or not it was a fascination is hard to
determine, but his new bearing pleased Oduna;
she believed him always in the right, and fought
his battles with a strange persistence. It may
have been that she saw in him qualities unrevealed
to others; at least, she believed him born for a

stormy and fateful life among his peers, and not
thus to waste his energies among peaceful men
and timid women. I do not know what spirit of
war and command came into the world with his
birth, and can only dream of what he might have
done had his fate been tried on heroic fields. Together the gloomy leader and his yielding bride
were drifting away from the little company; more
and more they talked alone, and sadder grew the
face of the father, who now believed he had fore-
seen all this from the first. He lost none of his
love for Oduna, but watched over her with jealous
care.

All days of their journey were much alike; indeed, the only variety was in the changing mood
of their half-feared leader. One day had seemed
longer than the others by his increased sullenness,
and the heart of the father had felt unusually
lonely as he watched Oduna clinging to her
estranged husband more closely than ever, as they
lingered just behind in the darkening shadows of
the oncoming twilight. The company, wandering
aimlessly, had stopped beside a small stream,
swollen by recent floods, thinking to camp for the
night, and hunt for a safer ford by the morning
light. But their now reckless leader urged them
to cross at once to the higher ground on the opposite shore.

His proposition met with such evident disapproval as to madden him He declared that he

would cross it to show them what cowards they were. The stream was narrow, and for this reason dangerous. But he would brook no interference, and turning to Oduna he commanded, with ringing voice, "Come with me."

For the first time she hesitated, and turned pale. She glanced up at her father, who shook his head, as if glad to test his power over her with her husband's.

"I dare not," she replied.

"I'll do the daring, you follow me."

The words were not harsh, but they were full of his native power, and I doubt if any man in the company would have dared stand still had he been addressed in the same way. Her father, hoping to settle the matter, pleaded that the horse was not a safe one, that water always made him frantic. Without answering he rode to her side, and with one arm lifted her to his knee. The very strength of his arm gave her such assurance that, had she looked into the very eyes of death, she would have had no fear. She leaned her head upon his shoulder, sobbing under the nervous strain, and the pain of her father's cold disapproval and astonishment.

The nervy horse, prancing as though eager for the struggle, plunged into the stream. Those on the shore were too surprised to make any resistance, and silently let them go splashing down into the river. It had deceived them all as to its depth and current. Long before the horse reached the center of the stream, they could see that it was being borne down by the current against its will. It was out of its depth, and could not swim against so strong a force, weighted as it was with its precious burden. Its quick pantings could be distinctly heard; snorts of fear were followed by a shriek of terror, terribly human, as it struggled madly with the stream, keenly feeling its responsibility. All stood speechless, spellbound, save the father, who, running down the river, came abreast of the plunging horse. He could hear Oduna's moans above the noisy flow of the water. Calling to her in firm tones not to give up, he kept beside them. Suddenly they came to a bend in the river where the current rushed in close to the shore before shooting on down the long channel. The poor horse had been bravely fighting to keep its feet down, but this sudden change in the course of the river sent it side-long to the shore. The riders still clung to the saddle-straps. The night had come on swiftly; out of the parting clouds shone the early moon, and its soft gleams wreathed about the white face of the soldier-boy, so loved, so feared, a halo of silvery light his only chaplet, as he fought with death, an unequal battle, not for himself, but for his loved Oduna.

To the father he seemed to grow cowardly weak, but the gray eye-witness who told me the story, said he believed the boy's heart burst with the awful fight, for, in an instant his arm relaxed, and he slipped away from the shore and his beautiful wife as silently and as swiftly as an arrow from the bow. Oduna, unconscious of her husband's fate, after an instant loosed her hold, and with a moan threw up her white hands as if praying for help; rising and falling on the waves, she sank once, twice, then rose again a little farther down the river.

The friends had gathered near the spot by this time, distraught by their powerlessness to help. The desperate father alone grasped the situation. He saw that she had been thrown towards the shore, and leaped in fearlessly. He struck his head against a jutting rock. So intense was his emotion that he imagined the shock to be merely the force of the water. He bore the scar always. As he came up he clutched at and finally grasped an overhanging limb, just within his reach, on account of the high water. From it he could reach the white hand beating despairingly against the water. He drew his lost child near him until together they were helped ashore.

As he lifted her from the water, it seemed to cling to her, and gurgle about the spot where last it held her, as hounds moan and sigh over a lost trail.

The night was a long and a dreary one with its watching and its loss. The camp missed its fierce and moody leader.

By dawn Oduna was able to ride in one of the covered wagons, propped up with pillows. But how pale was her face, how sad her eyes, no word can tell, for the black steed and its rider, her proud, daring soldier-boy, had gone with the cruel current to the ocean, where haply he would find some point of equipoise in mid-sea, and rest at last in horrible calm, as do sunken vessels.

It seemed to Oduna that her heart had washed out to some great ocean and was hanging in a calm, to break which would be the happiest relief. No tears, no words, no rest, nothing above, nothing beneath, nothing about her, yet held by some intangible force, and crushed with it all.

Ere long they reached their destination on the Mississippi, where Oduna lay looking ever toward the great river. It seemed so majestically quiet in its great course.

It was late in the fall when her fatherless babe was born; the river was full of the fall floods, and its roar was sullen and incessant. It filled her with painful unrest; she had looked into the babe's face but a few times until, at last, with the river's increased noise and lashing, as it crept farther up the dikes, the deathly calm was broken, and in a breaking up of her heart's great fountains her soul went down the current of that other stream whose ocean is the Eternal, and where the calm is Rest.

The boy had always a sad look in his face, a

sad, far-away look. Little Oduna came to cheer him at last in his manhood, as she is now trying to cheer the old, old man out on the rock. To her life is glad, and the waves come dancing in like children at play; but to him the river's music is ever a sad wail of lost love and death.

It sobs, and his failing ears catch th sound coming in on every wave, "Oduna, Oduna," just as he had heard the soldier-boy cry out that night so long ago, when he was so cruelly parted from his bride; calling as if pleading for forgiveness for his overmasterful spirit, ere he should sink.

"Oduna, Oduna."

His tear-dimmed eyes see no white sail out on the river, only the black steed and the moon-kissed, white face of the soldier, for as the years have passed he has come to love the impetuous, brave lover of his lost Oduna, and to hold them both alike, watching for him beyond life's last sullen stream.

WHILE THERE IS LIFE THERE IS HOPE(?)

"Well, he's dead, my bebby is," she said bitterly, tearlessly. "Maybe it will sober Jim up for a day 'r two any how," trying to discover a crumb of comfort in her heart's famine.

Her name? It does not matter. She was a common, helpless scrub-woman in a tumbled-down tenement-house at the corner of Mulberry and Park streets, just off of the Bowery, with the ordinary drunken husband. Even in the vile Italian district, this haggish old ruin in which she lived seemed viler than its surroundings. With a rotten-odored grocery on the ground floor, and a stenching stable joining at the rear; sliced into by a narrow, slimy stairway, too dark and ugly to ascend—just the way down into some vampire's retreat; the air heavy with the decay of vegetables and meat on the stalls under the scorching sun, the only marvel was that the baby had lived the half of six months. Indeed when one studied the face and figure of the stoical mother, her mein, wild, hungry and hunted in spite of her assumed indifference, he wondered that that frail piece of

flesh which she called her "bebby" had ever
drawn a single breath.

One could at least heartily agree with the comforting neighbor who had dropped in, more because a death was an event even in that charnel
street, than through sympathy, when she said:

"Oh, well, it couldn't have lived through the
summer no way; better be dead now than cry another whole month."

And the mother sadly replied, " Yes, that's so."

I wish I could bring this house into your sight.
Its devil-fish owner had evidently tried some years
before to jest with his conscience by having the
wide boards of the first story painted a light blue,
and the remainder of the building yellow trimmed
with red. *A harlequin in a vault.* He should
have painted it iron grey, with huge skull and
cross-bones on the front and sides. Dante alone
could have designed for the rear.

I climbed with a friend to its attic, one hot July
day, having observed the notice, " rooms to let,"
on the stair-post. Of a sweet-faced old lady with
a mixed, foreign accent, I learned that the eight or
ten feet square under a sloping ceiling, with a single little triangle of light at one end, could be had
for five dollars a month. She paid five and a half
for hers just across the little, narrow hallway, but
her daughter's family occupied it with her.

The devil is not long in taking the cue from his

imps. We shall hear yet that apartments in hell are being let at so much a month.

But to my story. I do not know how this American mother came to be down on this extreme foreign level. There she was, and will sink lower, doubtless, until she strikes bottom at last, with us all, in the grave. No, I forgot. Hers will be in Potter's Field. So have we challenged the Leveller himself. Have we? I fancy I hear him laugh.

She was tall, but stooped; half her teeth were gone; eyes far back in their sockets; the nose thin; ears transparent, but yellowish. In dark blue veins her blood lay stagnant. Only a poor skeleton, its joints held in place by chaffed skin. The labor-saving machine of a brutal husband, the slave of his ungratified passions, the unwilling mother of his eight, scrawny, nervous, incapable children. The oldest was a boy, already a drunkard; the next a girl of seventeen, into whose eyes the last two weeks had brought the hunted look, so common, so pitiful, the precursor of the brazen stare and bold invitation.

Can't you take the scorn out of your soul and say with her over her dead "bebby," "Yes, that's so?"

She took it finally from the ragged comforter on the floor, and laid it on the only table in the room.

"I oughtn't to lay it up there," she said, "Jim won't like it, when he comes in. But I don't know what else to do. The children 'll be fightin' in a minute, and like as not fall all over it. Well, I reckon they'll be glad enough it's gone, it's been a sight o' trouble to 'em."

The inventive genius, or rather the memory of the half-kind neighbor, suggested a way out of the difficulty. She brought the single chair from her own room, and putting it with its rickety mate, laid the wash-board upon them, and rather tenderly placed the now stiff body upon this improvised bier.

For one day at least that board must lie idle. It had torn the mother's fingers' ends so many hard days, and now she could never look at it again without a deeper hurt.

"There," she said, "I guess that'll do. No, you needn't undress it, it ain't got anything but that one slip. I wish it was cleaner, but nobody'll see it, I guess. Here is a handkerchief I left out of the washing last week; I will put it over its little face. I can't get its eyes shut."

"They say they's in purgatory for some reason or nother when they act like that," said the neighbor, who was a devout Catholic in times of trouble. "Has it ever been baptized?"

"No. I've come to have my doubts whether they have any souls or not—bebbies or men."

"God forgive ye," cried the other, crossing herself superstitiously.

"Well, I am sure He don't treat us much as though He thought we had any."

With a dead baby in the house, and not a crust in the cupboard; with a drunken husband without, and a gnawing pain within, the heart can doubt with little effort, especially if it has believed the dogma that an inscrutable providence orders every particular event of every particular life, with a particular purpose for that life.

Did you ever try to analyze a soul? Try it now. Here is a hungry woman; she has not laughed for years; has sung no hymn, had no altar of prayer, not even a secret closet. Her love for her children has been animal, not human. She has no great ambition for their future—only a horrible fear. No training of souls toward ideals—she has lost her own. No visions come to her of old age in the arms of her beloved—even now they are strangers. She trembles before her husband; she even stubbornly protested against her babe's robbing her of her life blood for its food. If she thinks of God at all, it is with clinched hand; if of death, it is to crave it, even with Hell—it surely cannot be worse than this, she thinks.

Take her hand, put it on the frozen snow of her baby's cheek; draw her down gently till her lips are blistered with its death-frost; with a word, set her whole frame a-quiver with nervous agony. Start the echoes of her youth vibrating through the empty chambers of her impoverished soul, till

the night comes on. Watch with her by the flickering light of the dim candle, whose shadows move
like restless ghosts in the grim corners of the
attic death-room. Keep your wide-opened eyes,
nervously strained, intent upon her face, while she
sleeps a moment, even under the dread expectancy
of her husband's drunken cough; see the shadows
come and go on her quiet face, so faint beside the
deep, black shadows on her soul, as in fitful dream
she looks back, and beyond, and forgets the present. Sit and watch till the morning. Then if you
can keep scornful, and reproachful, and accusing,
your soul is already *damned* under that Divine
law, "Inasmuch as ye did it not unto one of the
least of these, ye did it not to me. Depart from
me, ye *accursed.*"

Have you ever analyzed a soul?

Your own?

Across the street, an unclean Italian, with distressing cries, is calling his little circle of patrons
to his stall to celebrate the cutting of a half-
decayed melon. He shares with them for a
"penny a slice." Half-naked children at the
breast, or screaming at their mother's skirts,
pledge the continuance of human misery for at
least another generation. Fakirs stand at every
twenty feet with wares to tickle the fancy of silly
youths and maidens. A street of commerce to
turn one's heart sick if he did not see the exact

counterpart, enlarged, on Broadway. The same
strife and noise, curses and blows, lying speech
and chuckling glee over ill-gotten gains—the only
addition, dignified concealment. Then is the
heart sick indeed.

But the babe sleeps—would God the mother
slept, too, the same long, unbroken, dreamless
sleep. But at last the stupor nature so kindly
furnishes when the death-blow strikes one, begins
to disappear. Every nerve is trembling, her face
is twitching, objects quiver before her eyes, her
ears are throbbing with the heavy tread of the
creaking stairs.

"Jim is comin'," she gasps to the now sympathetic neighbor. "Don't go! help me! He'll say
I've killed it."

But a worse trial is before her. Jim has heard
on the way from the shop that his baby is dead.
He had been waiting for work all day. No money,
no credit, no liquor, no hope. Weak and nervous,
he stumbles up the rickety stairway, like the
ruined, frightened, helpless, hopeless man he is.
What ancestry failed to do for his wrecking, alco-
hol has supplemented. No curses, no blows;
nothing but self-condemnation, self-beatings. . She
could have endured blows better than these.

The weakness of a broken body; the more terrible weakness of a reeling reason, is upon him.
The reaction is such as none but lost and depraved
men can know. It is a species of insanity. Per-

haps the Compassionate One counts it often as the last effort of wretched souls toward sanity.

"My God, Mary, where is the bebby? Jack said it was dead. I told him he lied. He said it starved to death. And then I called him a d——d • liar. Where is the little clover? There, I thought I heard it cry. I don't know, mebby I'm drunk agin. No, not a glass to-day; haven't got a red to my name. Pull that curtain back and let me see my little chick. God! what's them chairs doin' there? Why, you have been crying child. What's wrong? I feel all run down myself."

"Look, what yer doing, Jim?" the mother cried, as he grasped one of the chairs to sit down, "don't you see the bebby is there?"

She fell to the floor in a death-like swoon; the strain had been too long, the struggle too hard. Her only chance for life, however, had come in this enforced rest.

But no such rest came upon Jim. As he stooped to examine the half-covered board a corner of the white handkerchief lifted with the light current of air stirring through the window. The white face with its unclosed eyes lay before him like a frozen passion, the hot, consuming passion of his life; all his passions in ice. He shivered like one called in the dead of night, by some one unseen, in a haunted house. Then he burned with the fever of the plague. Falling upon his knees he crooned be-

15

tween his sobs such wailing words as soothsayers might envy, but no life returned.

"Oh, my precious clover, my hungry bebby; poor little starved bebby; pa's boy. So cold, and my head so hot; mebbe I kin warm you. God, how cold! Come, I'll hold you, oh, so tight. Oh, I can't bend its arm around my neck any more, it's so stiff; what shall I do? Wake up, Mary, quick, the bebby's hungry. He don't like his pa any more, he wants you."

In the meantime the crying neighbors had resuscitated the poor mother, whose pain was just beginning its real throbs. She lay like a corpse in form, but never so sensitive to every sound, every motion as now. Her long fingers were nervously twisting the untidy sheet thrown over her. For an instant she did hear her babe, she did feel it in her arms, alive and happy, so near did she draw to the wavy line where the finite merges into the Infinite.

But that wail from across the room: "Come, Mary, take the baby, he don't seem to know me any more," held her on this side.

Through the night and the next day the mother lay unnaturally calm upon the rough bed piled in the corner; lay watching every movement of friend and stranger alike. Her great hollow eyes followed wherever any one turned. She made no other sign, except when some one approached the spot where her baby lay. Then invariably she rose upon one arm and with heaving breast seemed just about to speak.

You have watched a mother-cat keeping silent guard over her dead kitten? The same animal instinct was here, pitiful and smiting. Once when a kind Sister of Charity came by invitation of the Catholic neighbor, and put her hand on the child's face, as one accustomed to the dead is apt to do in search for some lingering warmth which is never found, she gave a faint little scream, and would have crawled from the bed if others had not restrained her.

The other children, dressed in the only whole clothes the entire house could afford, gathered in from the various families' scant wardrobes, drew no attention from her. She did not see them. When no one was moving she would turn herself so she could look at Jim. Without stirring, for half an hour, she would keep her eyes upon him. There may have been a slight delirium, just enough to calm her, as is frequently the case, but I believe the poor woman knew all that had happened. The mystifying veil had been rudely rent. She saw all. Her difficulty lay in solving the problem. Her weak brain was lost in the maze of these inexplicable facts.

It was just the reverse with Jim. Not the problem, but the facts troubled him. A pauper, a drunkard, and a dead child in the house—his own child; starved to death, and to be laid to-morrow in Potter's

Field. These the elements; these and an awful
pain, a hideous remorse, a dread of the future.
All the first night he moaned, with occasional
spasms of grief. When once he realized that the
child was dead, he did not go near it again. He
avoided that part of the room, even with his eyes.
A crushing horror had possession of him. I believe he would have died of nervous fear had he
been compelled to touch the dead body again. In
his changing moods he would talk it all over with
some of the men as they tiptoed in with awkward
embarrassment, hat in hand: the lowest will not
stand covered in the presence of death. Talked of
how he had been away all day; hadn't known the
baby was very sick; had been out of luck lately,
and guessed this was part of the game. Everybody seemed dead against him. Then the grief
would come again. Fortunately no one had asked
him to drink during the day. He may have
thought of it a few times himself; but why? He
hadn't a cent.

The Associated Charities Committee had been
informed of the case and had the funeral in
charge. It was announced through the house for
ten o'clock the following day. The second night
passed, bringing a little rest to the tired ones;
then came the trying day. No matter how resigned one may become, and philosophical, the
funeral hour of his beloved will open the wound
afresh. The silent friends gathering in; harsh

footfalls breaking the awful stillness; the quickening of the heart under the final emotion. How familiar!

It happened that Dr. Goodwest, a visitor in the city at the great Christian Endeavor Convention, was in conversation with a member of the Charities Committee early in the morning of this funeral day concerning the work of the Society, and was invited to attend the services that his own eyes might be better witnesses for him than the words of others. Standing, a dozen of them, in that crowded little attic chamber, the good doctor was moved beyond measure by what he saw. It was all new and strange to him; he had only read of such scenes; that he should be a part of one, affected him beyond anything he had ever known. He was asked to pray. I trust the reader will permit me to record that prayer here, as it is in heaven.

Jim was sobbing; the mother, propped up with old garments, lay panting on the bed, close to which the doctor stood. He lost his ordinary reckonings, this great-souled man. He knew nothing but that a man and woman were undone, and that God is a Healer.

" Great Father, thou lovest all thy children, but best of all, thy little, weak, helpless, smitten children. Thou wouldst not hurt a sparrow, but wouldst notice even its fall. Surely, then, Thou wouldst not hurt these dear souls of Thine, these

sick, hungry, naked, and imprisoned little ones of
our dear Lord.   Jesus, who came to heal, to seek
and to save the lost, could not love Thee nor obey
Thee unto death, if Thou wast not the God of
Love.   In the change of things here, pain and
death come.   But over them all Jesus has
triumphed.   Oh, God of mercy, bind up this man's
hurt, for he is wounded of nature and of Satan.
In Thee alone is his help.   This poor woman, oh,
Thou Son of Mary, do Thou be her Son, her Brother, her All.   This little babe sleeps in thy tender
arms, to waken in sinless Eden.   Keep these and
us unto that same end.   By Mary's forgiven sins,
by the prodigal son's tears, I pray thee forgive, and
restore, and save, even by this loss, this man, this
woman, unto eternal life.   It is of Thee, oh, Christ,
I ask it.   Amen."

No anguished cries followed these lofty words,
as is so often the case where ignorant comforters
talk of God's heavy, chastening hand.   A calm,
a Galilean quiet fell upon those ignorant lis-
teners under the tenderness and earnestness of his
musical voice.   Where they failed to follow the
word, the spirit of his prayer moved them.   No
sermon followed, fortunately, though one had been
suggested by a member of the committee.   The
doctor went over to Jim's side and putting his magnetic hand on his bent shoulder filled him with
new strength.   He did not say : " Your child is
in heaven ;" " It was best for it to die now ;" or,

"be resigned to the inscrutable mysteries of Providence." How gratefully I record it! he said infinitely more. This is what he said:

"You will be sick, my dear man. You must come away with me now. The friends will see that everything is done just right; I have a plan to propose to you for the future." To the mother, who needed kindness more than words, he simply said: "Don't get up. Let these good people look after you. You need a little rest. All will be well."

After the little procession had moved slowly down the stairs, Dr. Goodwest took Jim by the arm and started on his mission. As they passed up the Bowery, the great, surging, stolid, dull-eyed crowd, well-nigh froze the hope in his heart. Which way blew the winds, which way coursed the tides? The sea was fathomless, the swimmer faint and worn; the man overboard was far from being rescued. In a quieter spot they waited for an up-town car.

He had begun right, and had he possessed the power would have finished this man's reformation, in all probability; but as yet all such efforts find one man pulling at the oar while a steady, relentless current of public opinion and public indifference is pushing him down toward the gulf.

A score of questions flooded into utterance. How long had it been since Jim left his last place of work, and for what reason? What plans had

he now, and where had he tried for work? Had
he any friends who could help him? What were
his average earnings when sober, and how often
did he become intoxicated? They were like flashing saber-stabs upon a cotton ball. "The black
list," and "Pat Rooney's Place," were the only
intelligible responses. There was nothing in his
replies calculated to melt ice.

The good Doctor was following an impulse
which in his western home might have led to success. Had he personally conducted any one, however unpromising, to one of his several parishion-
ers who employed men, with a request for his
employment, his petition would have been immediately granted, out of respect for the Doctor, and
because there is less organization among employ-
ers West. He had a single hope now. An old-
time friend of his was a large manufacturer in a
Brooklyn suburb. He would present Jim at the
city office, and ask for aid for friendship's sake.

He scarcely stopped to think that should this
succeed, there were ten thousand other hopeless,
helpless, heredity-smitten, soul-killed men for
whom there was no pitying Dr. Goodwest.

The greetings were made as brief as possible,
for his energies were always direct or nothing.

"Nothing would please me more than to help
you, Doctor," with the emphasis upon the you. "I
will have him looked up, and if he is not on the
black-list I will try him a week."

"But he is on the list," pleadingly broke in the minister.

"That settles it. I am powerless. We must protect one another. We would soon become the prey of designing and thieving tramps, whose delight would be the destruction of our property and doubtless our lives. Let him keep sober, learn to be thrifty and keep out of trouble. Every man has his chance. If he loses it he must not blame you and me, Doctor."

The Doctor made no reply; his heart was too full, and his thoughts too hot.

He kept thinking: "Why not make his clerk read Homer; why not open the insane asylums and flog the inmates for their lost chances."

"I wrote my check yesterday for a cool thousand to build a mission church adjoining my works. I do not say it to boast, but that you may understand me. That is the only way to help these people, and that is confounded slow."

Dr. Goodwest arose respectfully, and without reply withdrew with his burden. They stood a moment on the curbstone of the city's greatest thoroughfare. "What shall I do with him?" came rushing into his consciousness. His home desolate; his wife a hopeless invalid, soon to become a mother again; his children ruined already before learning what sin really is; the passion for drink being even then in his restless eyes; distrustful of every soul—the Doctor can feel a gulf sinking between them deeper every moment. No work but the lowest sort of drudgery, an hour at a time. No ambition, nothing to appeal to but his animal affection for his dead child, and even that has turned to horror.

The indifferent crowd hurried by, some with rude jostling and half-muttered imprecation. Each face knotted in selfish thought of to-morrow, or open with careless mirth. As a rising tide eddies and courses about a black rock on the shore line, and at last covers it from sight, so threatened this thoughtless, irresistible tide of humanity.

"My God, what shall I do with this poor wretch?" unconsciously cried the man of mercy aloud.

"I'm dummed if I know," came in swaggering indifference from the man at his side, fast slipping back into the sea.

What would you have done?

A SOUL'S RESURRECTION.

I wonder what fate has against me now; what old score is she about to settle? That of all times, this day should be heavy with mists and clouds, goes beyond my usual shrewdness in interpreting her moods. As if to make her victory complete she lashed me into unrest with horrible dreams through the whole night. Dreams of sins of which she declared my youth—the only gleam in all this shadow of a doomed life—had been guilty; and she further declared with her accustomed shriek, that like scars on the face of one we love, made by our own demoniac temper, so should these sins come ever before me; not distinct, like so many demons, with hateful leer, to taunt me, but in the hurts and unhealed wounds of my friends their grinning heads should pop up, stained with clotted blood, and mocking, disappear, leaving a flame whose distressing odor should vex when mine eyes, no longer able to see them through their film of disease, should be blind!

I am sore with vain tossings to turn away from the sad and reproachful eyes of those I once have loved, and do still remember when my own sorrows

will let me. Me, they have forgotten; from their
sight I have sunk forever; I could hate them
for it with a poisoning hatred.

At last exhausted with mind-racings up and
down the narrow cell of my dream-prison, I awoke,
while a loud crash of thunder made my already
quivering nerves jerk with pain. This day was to
have been the birthday of a new purpose. An
energy of body and soul, to goad myself into motion out of my environment, had been the plan for
this half-cycle of the earth. How this old sun-curs-
ed planet goes on maddened to its doom! I verily
believe I should like to be alive the day it goes
crushing against some burnt-out sun, and is dashed
into atoms, if only this wrecked brain could be
crushed too; but what if some thought should live
on apart from the brain that created it—horrible
possibility! I had infinitely rather be this rotten-
ing brain, sure to crumble ere long, than to be any
thought of my last ten years, and eternal!

I do entreat thee, thou great force, somewhere,
everywhere, let me live not; not even in thought; annihilate, annihilate, leave no atom, no purpose, no
longing anywhere inwrought with my personality!
I want to die, I will die! What was that? Must I
dream of the accursed devils with my eyes wide open?
Is there no smiting, fate-detaining, no untrembling
hand? My soul cowers like a whipped cur. Soul?
Ha, ha! Come hither, thou subtle trickster. If
thou art, let me conjure thee forth where mine eyes

may behold thee. Ah, shame-faced, thou hidest deeper still! I get no pulse of thy life. Thou art not. Gods! what a crash was that. Even the heavens are breaking with their weight of woe. The roar of the sea is lost in the tempest thunder. The window is veiled with a sheet of rain. The air is close. My heart has quit beating, and trembles, as though about to say farewell to its wretched house. Is there no help? Can no one hear my cries? Must I perish alone? Save me; Zeus, Almighty, save—ah! down! A baby's puny wails are not so pitiful. No more tricks like that, or I'll give thee to elemental clay, thou old barnacled hulk of worn-out passions. But that this, of all days, should be so hellishly dark! To-day, when the friend of my youth is to greet me! Here is the crumpled note now, where I flung it in my rage last night. " By to-morrow's sunset I will see your face once more!" My face; bah! Where is that cracked mirror, the only thing in the universe that dares face me. Here, you accursed revealer, show me perdition's grim features once more. How my hand trembles! My face; yellow, wrinkled, soulless. Yes, it is my face. Oh, that sudden pain; was it in my flesh or in my spirit? After all, are they not the same? A thought came with it, whatever its source; the demons peering from some gaping wound might magnetize my blood with their poisoned eyes until I should turn to a stone. (That miserable dream.) What a monu-

ment of human folly would my poor body make,
petrified, and set upon a pedestal on some great
thoroughfare, where the mighty multitude, pushing on to its unconscious doom, should jeer at my
ruins, not knowing that they were prophetic of
their own !

I shall be helpless by sunset ; sunset—how like
the olden times is that word ! He was a poet then,
my lost Raphael. We stood on many a hill together and sighed with sleepy nature as she shut
her eyes in the soothing twilight. I loved him, I
don't know why. Strange that one man should
love another, in this heartless age. But I did.
My heart and eyes moved with the rhythm of his
speech. But his hand let mine go one day, to take
the warm, responsive hand of one he loved from
that instant better than he did me. My soul
cried out, and my face spoke a silent language my
lips refused to utter, as I let him pass away, pleading with me, but not restored. Ah ! I thought I
heard a laugh. Who would dare pierce this
gloom with a dart of light. There again ; but no
sunlight is in it, only the chill of the moon. Ah !
the demons ! Why should I have had that dream?

"See my face once more and grasp my hand ; "
my hand ; see how it shakes, it pricks as though
with nettles ; I wonder if it will sting his touch,
and poison him ?

What if he should laugh like the imps ; what if
he came to mock me in my weakness ! I would

strangle—no, he had a kind heart always, and despite my cloudiness, shone at me as if he meant to melt away my coldness. If only the day had been fresh and bright for me, I might have started the old rusty wheels again. But I fear my power is gone. Another hand might. But what hand? I dare not try it, and yet, just one touch might be like a charm to set in motion—no, no, it is too late. I must submit.

A diseased, death-stricken child must indict its generator, when its mind turns logical, for the crime of its suffering; and if it shall hate him at last, the syllogism shall be nearer perfect. What then shall be the emotion of a race of children toward their common Father (according to the theologues), if every breath is accompanied with intense pain? What infinite imperfections, what diseased vitals must afflict Him, the Creator, that such an inheritance has fallen to his creatures. To be sure, the poets and theologians speak in rather disparaging terms of our Mother Earth, and pour out on her frail head the vials of their unseemly wrath, and insinuate unblushingly that scandals innumerable have blackened her fair name, while to our generator, which after an ancient custom, they name God, they impute all virtues and excellences. With sly thrusts and declamatory denunciations, they seek to pile upon her bony shoulders, weakened as she is by overmuch maternity, the responsibility of all the in-

herited diseases of body and soul, together with
all acquired ones, and not a few imaginary ones
in their "unbelieving" neighbors. As usual, fem-
inine weakness has not dared to refute these
charges except in an occasional cyclone or vol-
cano, when so black grows her placid features, so
fiery her temper, that even I am led to suspect her
usual smiles and pleasing moods, as being a sort
of coquetry—innocent, doubtless, and an involun-
tary condition of her sex! And, I am more than
puzzled, when in the midst of her choicest favors
and bestowals, she suddenly turns away and hides
her face under her spotless veil of white, pouting
in freezing silence, her very tears turning to ice-
drops, when lately they were warm and pleading.
And worse than all, I am certain that while she
dashes our love for her with sleety floods, double-
faced, she flames with immodest lust towards those
who are gathered at her side away from us, until
in the tropics, life shoots up in supreme and waste-
ful rankness and profusion. Moody, passionate,
promising, but not fulfilling, generous to a fault
when inclined, or selfish, cold, destructive in tempest and fire,—what if after all, the poets and
preachers are right! Her children resemble her
somewhat, I must own.

But it cannot be the truth, or the preachers never
could have hit upon it. I am convinced, and any
sound mind ought to be.

Moreover I make answer to these half truths, by

quoting the preacher's own Book of facts (?): "God made man, and breathed into him the breath of life, and he became a living spirit." That should end the dispute and forever settle the origin of these pains, convulsions and fears. No God would do the like; but such conditions do exist, therefore there is no God. As a matter of course, the pulpitarian replies with his usual bravado and intimidation, that the same Book declares, "God made man out of the dust of the earth."

Well, what if he did? What has that to do with it? There was no life until the breathing took place, and the breather is responsible for all that has resulted from that breathing. See the folly of their argument; any one but a bigoted theologian would discover that it leads directly to evolution, and he dare not advocate that because of a slight financial embarrassment which might ensue professionally. I only wish that he might get entangled in that net, he and all his kind; for of all nonsensical, sentimental trumpery, to my mind, Evolution is the airiest. It proves too much. It proves an intelligent beginning, and a providential continuing and developing. It proves, too, an adequate destiny as the certain end of this growth. Admit these legitimate demands of Evolution, and you admit the preacher's wildest assertions.

There is no growth, because there was no intel-

16

ligent beginning; there can be no destiny! A germ sprouts only when it happens to fall into the environment its nature needs. One dare not say his own life is the result of any plan—merest chance. He finds his whole nature is pre-determined by pre-natal influences over which he had no control.

The sun happens to shine against a cloud as the rain falls, and the rainbow appears, just as at this instant it spans the eastern sky yonder.

At last the sun is coming. How have I gotten through this day? For an hour I had forgotten the night and its visions. But the setting sun reminds me that my visitor will soon arrive. What a mood is this for receiving one who years ago belonged to the inner circle. How the years have piled the mountains between us. I am told he has found the delight of his earlier ambitions in much success and applause. It is well. I seem to have stood still on the same spot where we parted, except that I have been slowly sinking. Perhaps he may give me a hand; but no, I will not have it so! Let him keep his woman's philosophy. I want none of it. I am myself, and if I sink, it will be into oblivion; but will it be into forgetfulness? To that question I get no answer. Oh, the pain, and the demons again! Did I then so wrong my old friend that his return persists in bringing to my memory a sin half forgotten?

But see the budding sunset blooming into its

full flower. A perfect garden of color and form. And the sea is at his flattery again. He takes on the mood of the sky, and throwing himself into wooing the graceful queen of the air, wins her almost to his arms, the white drapery of her beauful garments sinking down until the highest waves kiss them. As she looks longingly down, beholding her imaged self in the sea's embrace, she abandons herself to the delights of her imagination. But this is all. The law of each holds them apart, and they may only wish and dream. God! this maddening law which. separates! So my youthful fancy lived and loved in vain. My love, her own sweet answer with promised favors gave, but Fate shook his hoary locks about his stern, accursed face with his emphatic denials. I dare not count how many black figures in my life's sum are due to this denial. How many long hours, hopeless, bringing forth their dark-visaged brood to trouble me and my kind; how much discontent and hatred!

How they border in lines not easily seen, these two realms of hate and love. When one sets his heart into pulses of love, the twitch of a single nerve may change it to hate. I hated, not her lost self, but the world, men, women, and even innocent children, the days, the race, because of the aid they rendered Fate against me so gratuitously. Alas! as I recall it now, it was because of this that first I distrusted my heart's charm and solace,

that friend whose presence just now seems to draw
nigh, like an influence one feels but does not see.

A step at last.   How the old porch creaks under
his steady tramp!   Perhaps some evil spirit is
exorcised by his coming.   Aha, the old knocker
has fallen off!   His bare hand will knock at my
portal—oh, what emotions!   am I so weak then—
what and he should beat at my poor heart with
his bare hand.   Could I refuse him?   Fie, art thou
craven then?   Down; a child's heart could be less
simple.
Yes; a firm knock was that.
I believe I can stand.
"Come in, my—come in, I say."   How unnat-
ural I feel.   "Why is this, dear me, how much
you have—no, not changed, but grown, I was
about to say.   Oh, excuse me, I am very feeble
to-day.   I must sit down; be seated, do.   I
scarcely—, you seem to be something more than
the old Raphael of Yarrow.   Oh yes, I know.
Don't refer to them.   There are years and years.
I have one, you the other.   Sorry to see me so
feeble?   Oh, yes, I am feeble; it's my ill health.
I, well you see, hard work in the laboratory, and
all that.   But let us to your work.   I can see in
your face that all I have heard is true.   The ex-
travagances of your friends?   Oh, no, you must
allow me; I feel stronger than for days, it really

does me good through and through to see you
again. You knew me at the first glance? Well, I
was afraid you might not. You know we old ras-
cals don't like to be thought changing much.
Younger than you? Impossible! Yes, I remember now. Oh, yes, of course, ill health, that
accounts for it; you are right. Make me young
again? Well, I wish you might. But can you
recall all—enough of that, however?

"Tell me of the years since we parted. Your
mother dead? Alas, how it presses upon us all;
and no, not Eleanor, your wife! She dead, can it
be? And you live still and smile? Resignation?
There is none, it is only an iron will, stronger than
emotions. I never had it. It makes me bitter to
think of it.

"But then the years have brought you compensation. Ah, what did you say? I was thinking
of that day; go on."

"Such compensation," my friend replied, "as
only sacrifice, and the unexpected both in joy and
in sorrow bring. Through sorrow and unceasing
pain have I come to what I have. God hath so
led me."

"God—yes—well, you know I am not what we
were then. Perhaps my sufferings may have done
it. But the old ideas of Providence are all in
ruins in my brain."

"I will not say my own have not changed since
our youthful speculations. It does not seem to me

that God stops natural law for the individual, but makes the individual the instinctive, intelligent subject of laws which do not vary; but in their invariableness is our protection and sole safety. Yet I do believe that His spiritual Kingship can make any physical calamity which our disobedience brings upon us, lose much of its force, when by it we come in line with His purposes. For example, a misstep may lame me for life in spite of God; but as a cripple I may, in accord with His thought, and by His grace, be more in this present life than I could otherwise have been, and better adapted to the environment of the life to come. But I am wearying you."

"No, indeed," was the quick answer; "this seems new to me, and refreshing, after this long fever-time. My temples have throbbed with the pain of angry thought so long, that your very tones seem like a gentle touch."

"I am not sure but that pain is to be the saviour of the world. You know we had great boyish conceptions of an ideal life in the days of our youth. Somewhere in the world there were heights cloud-wrapt and commanding. Upon these we were to stand. Just how, we did not know; certainly not by climbing; that was much too antique a way of ascent. We fairly believed some ingenious elevator system would present itself for our service. But I learned before many days that it was a long, long tramp to the foot of the mountain, and toilsome, exhausting climbing even to moderate cliffs from which one might get a wider horizon, while its summit seemed to lift itself into the snows more rapidly than I could climb. Since then I have been content, in some . measure, to remain where my strength can carry me."

"Ah, yes, and I; I frantically beat and tore my poor hands against barriers giants could not re- move, bitterly, accusingly, until the pain struck to my heart, and I slipped down from the position I had gained, nerveless, to the very beginning, and too weak to attempt it again. I have had the pain, too ; tell me why it should bless you and curse me ? Answer me—you seem to know all. Oh, my friend, I beg of you not to heed me, I am beside myself. Forget such words as these. But the mystery is so baffling."

"I can only reply that my pain awakened my resistance to hindrances, and the experiences of the hardships of the day drew me closer to my friends and the All-Soul. I remember it now, though I had half forgotten then, that in the days that are now like a dream, the days of my boy- hood, I had much concern for the life of Mary's Son. My mother and I were reading together the story of His life. We had read as far as the gar- den-scene ; the Savior's rising up and bidding the sleeping disciples follow Him. I was separated from her for a few days, I do not remember why, nor does it matter now. I did not dare go on with the reading without her. I went about the house like one daft, and bereft of friends. I knew something of the incidents of the crucifixion, but had never read them in their historic connection. I was wondering what He would do next after the horrible pain. It was terrible to me that He should have been alone and neglected when He was craving sympathy. But He appeared so strong when He rose up that I adoringly worshiped Him in my boyish admiration. Then I tried to imagine what He would do next; and all I could think of was a host of angels besieging Him and begging Him to return with them, and not go forth on His dark, forsaken way. I can remember it now, the look of astonishment and grief that came upon His face as He turned to them, His hands hanging down by His side motionless. He said not a word, but such resolution was carved on His face that they withdrew at once; when all alone, leaving the disciples to follow on behind, He went out into the heavy darkness. It was a simple, childish fancy, but I learned that day what pain can do, and how it makes heroes. I was feeling the separation from my mother sharply and somewhat rebelliously; that picture ever-recurring gave me resolution. I turned to my duties at once; I never forgot it."

"Simple and childish, you say, but reverent for a child. Ah, from the currents of another life

have you received such a faith, such a hope, than
have I received my distrusts. There is the rub.
Inheritance and environment, who can resist these!
Rather bid the straw resist the torrent, the leaf
rescue itself from the whirlpool. Better reprimand
the leafless oak for its rotten heart, than one of
my mold and shape for disbelief and distrust.

"I have fought in this very room with the
demons that curse me. These windows rattle now
with my shrieks, and the trembling of mad tramp-
ing is still upon the floor. This has been my
grave, and I have struggled like one who comes to
life in his clay-weighted coffin, tearing out his
snaky hair, and cramping his joints until his
bones snap like reeds, and with bursting eyes
struggles to be free, to breathe! Here I slowly
smothered, and felt my heart stopping; it is my
birthright. Explain it if you can."

"I will not attempt it, my dear friend; my heart
goes out to you with all the old-time affection.
You were ever a strange boy and man. But do
you remember the hunchback that brought our
not too plentiful linen from his mother's hut, at
the close of her ironing day? I see you do. He
was always repulsive to you. You have at least
heard of those articles in the *Quarterly Review*, on
the new philosophy of faith; they are the talk of
the thinking world, profound, sweet-toned and
helpful. I know them to be the work of our own
hunchback.

" Pain ? What can be more crushing than the jeers and insults of the men you meet, while you are dying already with the consciousness of your shame and disgrace. Add to these the whisky curse, poverty, lack of education ; and in spite of them all, the mind, the heart, genius victors ! There you read my answer to your question, and I beg you will not think it a harsh one."

" I had my ideals," came my evasive answer, " beautiful, inspiring. I was always a lover of the beautiful, and fairly revelled in the philosophy of nature's life and destiny. You were ever the better artist. But I had my ambition and promises as well. Why should I be cheated, while the hunchback, without a hope, without an ideal, probably, gained the full prize. I tell you it is all a damnable lottery ; it is fate. Set out towards what end you will, it is written in your very blood, upon your brain cells, whether or not you will ever reach it."

" I believe your mistake lies largely in the false notion of the beautiful and the ideal. As we look back towards the throne of the Cæsars, we exclaim, ' There has been but one life supremely beautiful.' It came out of the most despised community, and among an enslaved people. From the lowliest of the earth its outwardness, from the highest divinity its flaming inwardness. Its beauty lay in the interfitting of these two parts, and in its fitness with its environment. From the

summit of this spiral down to the chemical affinity
of atoms is the range of the ideal. Nor will the
quality suffer any change in the descent, no matter
how vast a gulf divide between any two embodi-
ments of it. The answer to the question, Why is
the Son of Mary beautiful, will answer the same
question in relation to the law of gravity. Har-
mony with its real environment, and the fulfillment of its destiny! And that not in a blind or
mechanical sense, but in a manner spontaneous,
natural, evolutionary. This makes individuality
the secret of life and motion. Every atom has its
unlikeness to all others, because of its peculiar
place and relation to other atoms—a peculiarity
no less marked by the Creator than that which
distinguishes between one man and another. I
am not sure but that sustained individuality will
be the eternal existence of which we dream. The
ability to sustain it by the overpowering life of
Deity, happy existence; the thrust upon and enforced sustainment by sin, unhappy existence.
The one will be perfect beauty, the other absolute
ugliness and deformity.

"The soul's only natural environment is spiritual
truth; spiritual presences collated about a central
individual and spirit force. The soul that by sin
shall be thrust into darkness, impurity and disin-
tegrating elements, is out of its environment, and
therefore unhappy.

"Again, it is the destiny of the soul to gain, at

first gradually, and afterwards absolutely, superiority over the body. This it does slowly under Christ here, and completely in the eternal life, at some stage of that life. It is not certain that the soul does not so adulterate itself with the physical habit of thought and love of this earth-life, to the degree that at its very best, it can only hope for absolute freedom at some remote period of the eternal existence, when the influence of the untainted Spirit over all shall have wrought in the soul its perfect work.

"But in the darkness and ruin which sin brings upon the soul after death, it is neither in its natural environment nor fulfilling its destiny; indeed the very opposite is true. Hence, there must be an utter lack of beauty! This is the definition of beauty, and the illustration of its meaning. But you got some foolish ideas in your head—do not think me unfriendly in this—which made you think yourself born for certain high ends and nothing less. It was the case with myself, I remember; it was the science of nature to which I proposed to devote my life; and I proposed to do it by rapid intuitions, half-revelations, which no one had yet known. You see how all this has changed. I have not the analytical mind, nor the classifying tendencies. I would soon have grown bitter in my disappointment and belabored fate. But I have been taught that one's work is that which he can do. Only thus have I been able to set in motion a small wave of happiness in the hearts of my friends."

"You mean to say, then, that I have missed my calling?"

"The most of the people we meet are dissatisfied, having had high ideals which were never realized. A smaller number, but larger than Matthew Arnold's 'remnant,' is stayed by Christian resignation, until they do not allow themselves to be very much surprised by, or disappointed over, any lot; while a very small number, and the smaller the better for us all, so wedded to their optimism, will declare everything to be just as they dreamed it, even after they have looked upon the reality. Their punctured bubbles never collapse, their saw-dust people never lose their graceful roundness. Hero worship has had not a little to do with our general estimates; we grant to a leader, a genius, all the virtues our imagination can conjure, more possibilities, in fact, than he himself ever dreamed of; much as some very imaginative people read into a poem a hundred things of which the poet himself was not conscious. It is very natural that when our worshiped heroes fail of the standard we set up, we should feel it keenly, and blame them for unsuspected weakness. Much of ancient and modern fiction has played no small part in the establishment of this habit. I remember you as a firm believer in the romancist's statement of life. Romance has its place in the domain of letters, but

not as the fashioner of our daily thoughts and
wishes.   Howells may not be far wrong when he
pronounces Tolstoi, the prince of realists, the greatest novelist of all ages.   I recognize the necessity
of a high standard of hoping and living ; that if we
were not capable of ideals, we would be with the
beasts ; that ambition is the fly-wheel of all life's
motion and achievement; that hope is a Divine
gift and keeps the heart ; that to the child, maturity
of thought and work is the ultima thule.   But is it
necessary that we set before us an unreasonable,
unattainable perfection in order that we may attain
some degree of perfection, though we do fall short
of the ideal?   Is it not a pernicious habit we have
fallen into, and does it not dwarf our lives at last ?
Is it necessary that the love-blinded swain shall
imagine every grace, every virtue, belongs to his
chosen, before he will run the risk of merging their
fortunes?   I wonder if sordid, money-loving, *mes-
alliance*-hating society has not unconsciously
wrought a good work in cultivating the habit of
walking into the matrimonial state with open eyes,
each conscious of the other's defects and shortcom-
ings.   Not to attain all is not to fail, nor does it
make any less the ideal toward which we struggled."

  "Your words seem wholesome, but under them
must be something that is false and deceptive ; my
own life marks them so."

  "Say rather, that you have made your life what

it is, by resisting both nature and God. She
moulded you in form for both strength and honor ;
the Infinite stood ready to fill you with a grace
Divine. But as a flower, had it will, might lay its
face on the black ground and turn its parched
mouth from the dew and rain, so did you. I would
God I might lift the flower back to the sun and
showers."

"Your words are gracious," I cried, my soul
all astir, "but to what end? It is like my old
dreams of heaven, to have you here by my side,
for it has been lonelier than death. No children's
tripping feet have ever crossed this bare floor, no
cheery voices have shaken the cobwebs of my
shadowed room, or of my deeper-shadowed brain.
No friend has for years entered into sincere
converse with me. Many have frowned, or smiled,
and passing the day, passed by. Not one has
stopped to say, 'Do you rest? Are you lonely?
May I come in?'

"None, till you came, have dared meet my doubting, scorning gaze. Like some sweet spirit you
have knelt at my ruined altar, and with your
human words smitten the dead rock of my hopes,
until a tiny stream begins to flow. But, no; there
is no hope. It is as though one blind were led to
the sea, and another should say, 'Look, behold
the vast deep, blue as the domed sky ; its waves
are coming in like frothing thoughts in a mad
chase. Look, do you not see its sublime, billowy

self?' And then the sightless sufferer should
say, 'No, no; I only hear a confusing roar, at first
holding and inspiring, then a booming and swish-
ing of waters at my feet that terrify me.' And
then like myself this moment, would cry out,
'Lead me away, haste, for the boom of the sea is
mixing with the sullen roar of my half-mad brain.
I cannot endure it.' No, no, my friend, it is beyond hope. The blind must see. Only a miracle
can do that."

"Just a word. By some strange freak of human nature we rush from superstition to atheism,
and back again to superstition. You think naught
but a miracle, like that given to the blind man of
Judea, will recover for you your inner sight. You
hang wholly on God's power and notion to give
you sight. Call back your reason and regard
yourself.

" Who came to this lonely spot of self-hate and
God-distrust ? "

" I, myself."

" Who loved it in spite of its pain ? "

" I."

" Who now talks of helpless blindness, conscious
of his condition ? "

" I."

" Who, but this instant, hopes and yearns for
the old life, the new life ? "

" I, myself."

" Then thou canst arise, and find Him of whom

thou knowest much in spite of thy gloom. Forgive me if I have been over-earnest, or seemed to urge myself upon you. But I felt, and do feel, that my soul's own brother cried to me in that pitiful prayer, and that I must help or die."

"Go on, go on. It is restful. It is like a good dream one dreams, and wakes, and dreams again. But it is only restful. One does not undo the convolutions of his brain-cells in an hour. The light does not come at the wish. But to see you, even dimly, in the shadows that have fallen around me, is a significant beginning. If ever it shall happen that I may lift up my earth-bound eyes, it will be not by some sudden and astonishing revelation, or inward work of grace or ungrace. It will be because I was able to see thee, thyself. I mean, to hear the tones of thy voice, feel thy presence, then afterwards to know one of the simplest truths perhaps, and then another, until at last I can take truth for truth's sake, and not thine and love's sake. At last it may happen, if I might hope for it, that I may discern another form, its outline against the eastern window—the window of the dawning; a form, upon which the sunlight may at last pour, revealing Him of whom you and your dead mother dreamed. What if I should close my eyes some night in your presence, in this so long demon-haunted room, and when I should awaken in the morning light I should behold His

17

presence in your stead, would there be any miracle
there? I think not; a natural development, not
in you, but in me. Ah, what fanciful dreams are
these? I cannot even rise from my chair alone; I
am broken, shattered, lost. You have given me a
glimpse of what might have been, but not now; it
is too late!"

"I like the high quality of your despair," my
friend returned in his musical tones. "It suits the
case well; you have named the only process by
which you may recover your mental health, and if
that be recovered, perchance your bodily health.
It will be by an evolution wrought by the warmth
and moisture of your friend's love, until the germ-
ing is over, then by adjusting yourself to your
environment. God speaks truth by men.

"I must ask you to say two words to-night before
we part. Words you have not uttered since those
early days, and not often then. Words by which
Divinity exists. Words which make men, by inheritance, sons of the Divine, and by grace, joint-
heirs with the older Brother. Words by which
life came, but they are not in all life. They are
not in all highest life, for the spirits of the Throne
have them not. They are the sign of humanity,
the soul of Divinity. They marked the hunchback from the most beautifully formed and graceful animal that ever started up from its forest concealment. They can remove you from yourself,
until your identity is wholly changed. They are

the secret of immortality, if I mistake not. They made the Man of Sorrows change his blood-sweat agony into God-like composure. They melt sin. They vanquish it. For the Great One does ever work in them when they are the echo of his own. He has uttered them ever since time first began, in every revelation. Men have no higher privilege than to echo them—not the echo of a hollow sound, not an earth-born cry, nor a demoniac shout—but an echo of the Divine. You know them, your destiny depends upon them. Will you say them? Dare you be silent now and live? Say them, my brother, my comrade of the hills, of the hopes of youth; by the love I bear thee still, say them!"

"I—I—I—WILL."

"Amen!"